MARK MANNOCK

Hell's Choir

A NICHOLAS SHARP THRILLER (3)

First published by Shotfire Books 2020

This novel is entirely a work of fiction. The names, characters and incidents portrayed in it are the work of the author's imagination. Any resemblance to actual persons, living or dead, events or localities is entirely coincidental.

First edition

ISBN: 978-0-6489036-2-8

This book was professionally typeset on Reedsy.
Find out more at reedsy.com

For Simon

Contents

Chapter 1

Now

There wasn't a sound. None at all. That was the trouble.

I coaxed my eyes open. An army of pain rampaged through my head, probing for more nerves to torture.

According to the blazing sun penetrating the window, it must have been morning. I'd been unconscious for at least ten hours. I'd put up a good fight the night before, but in the end, I was outnumbered and outclassed.

Now it was the silence—and the pain—that woke me.

Forcing myself out of bed, I threw on a pair of jeans and padded over to the hotel-room door. What I saw in the corridor was surprising—or rather, what I *didn't* see was the issue. No people, no housekeeping staff, no cleaning trolleys. Nothing. Midmorning in a busy international hotel. Something was not right.

I retreated into my room, tossed down some aspirin to calm my exploding head, put on a shirt and a pair of shoes, then headed back out into the passageway. There could be an innocent explanation, only somewhere in the back of my mind I feared otherwise.

The soft carpet cushioned underfoot as I strode toward the elevator area. I pressed the down button; it lit up. Reassuring. Eventually the elevator arrived. I stepped in and pressed G. Surely there'd be people on the ground floor who would know what was going on.

The elevator clunked to a stop. As the doors opened, I gazed expectantly across the crowded lobby—except that it wasn't. Not a soul in sight. There should have been guests, there should have been hotel staff behind the reception desk, and more than anything else there should have been Secret Service personnel at every door.

Shit.

Without thinking, I closed the elevator door, immediately pressing the tenth-floor button. Jefferson Blake had the entire floor reserved for his immediate entourage. Until that point, it hadn't occurred to me that Secret Service agents should also have been manning each elevator, ensuring that no one exited at Blake's floor. They weren't there. They weren't anywhere.

On the way up, I felt my nerves tense. Still, I prayed for a simple, logical solution. Maybe a bomb-threat evacuation. Fire alarm drill that I'd slept through? That could be it.

The light above the elevator door lit up the number ten. The ascending motion stopped. The doors slid open. As I looked across the hallway, I heard a sharp intake of breath. It was mine. At that same instant, any hope of a relaxing morning disappeared.

There were two Secret Service agents in view, both lying awkwardly on the floor. Taking three steps over to the first agent, I kneeled down and placed two fingers on his neck to check for a pulse. There was none. Without standing up, I turned and leaned toward the other agent, a woman. She was dead too.

A coldness enveloped me. It was a familiar feeling, the same as I experienced as a US Marine scout sniper when I laid eyes on a potential target. A professional needed to drain the emotional charge out of the moment. I was no longer a professional sniper, but some habits never leave you.

My Marine training took precedence over any instinct for survival as I charged along the corridor toward Jefferson Blake's room. I rounded the corner leading to his sealed off area and saw the four agents that should have been guarding his room splayed on the ground. I bolted passed them. There was no time to stop to check their health status. My primary concern was Blake.

The double doors of his suite smashed against the walls as I shoved my way through and raced down the short corridor that led to the principal living area. Two more agents were lying prone on the couch. Dead.

I scanned the rest of the room. A sprawling array of lounges and luxurious armchairs dominated the two separate sitting areas. Floor-to-ceiling windows ran the full length of the far wall, overlooking the city skyline. I almost smiled at the black grand piano perched extravagantly in the far corner. Almost. This was the most expensive and luxurious accommodation that you could find in the city of Khartoum, although that thought bore little relevance at that moment. Apart from the dead agents, there was no one else in sight.

The cold numbness continued to surge within me as I hurried from room to room, searching. I discovered two more bodies in the study; one slumped at a desk, the other on the carpet —probably departmental aides. At any moment, I was expecting to find Jefferson Blake's body.

I found no one else. Blake had disappeared.

Then the unimaginable hit me. I wanted to be wrong, but there could be only one explanation.

Someone had just kidnapped the vice president of the United States of America.

I double-checked each section of the suite before returning to the central room. Pulling my cell phone from my pocket, I sat on a couch. The one furthest from the dead agents. I dialed a number, but the line was dead. I was halfway through dialing a second time before I realized there was no signal. *Funny—I'd used my cell in this room two days ago.* I stood up and walked around. There was no signal anywhere.

I used the in-house phone to dial Jack Greatrex's room. It rang for a solid thirty seconds before a sleepy and exasperated voice answered. "What?"

"It's me, you need to get up to Blake's suite right now," I said, the agitation in my own voice evident.

"What I need is sleep."

"Jack, trust me, you want to be here, now," I replied.

"All right, if you say so, Nicholas. Will I need a pass to get through the Secret Service people?"

"That won't be a problem," I said. "Just get here."

Five minutes later, I'd rechecked each room twice more, searched under every bed and in every closet space. I was in the bathroom splashing some water on my face when I heard, "Holy crap."

I walked into the central room to see Greatrex staring at the two dead Secret Service agents on the lounge. The big fella appeared fatigued, bordering on disheveled. The preceding evening had been tough for both of us. On the other hand, the view confronting him was one hell of a wake-up call.

"Blake?" he asked.

"Nowhere to be found."

"Holy crap."

"You said that," I pointed out. "I've been downstairs, the lobby is empty."

"Secret Service?"

"Gone, no sign of them—at least none that are alive," I responded.

I studied my friend across the room, his forehead furrowed, eyes glowering. Greatrex and I had been to hell and back a hundred times over in the Marines and since. Frequently it was because of him that I made it back. Unsurprisingly, the concern on Greatrex's face mirrored my own.

Neither of us had any notion of what was going on here, but as the shock of the situation subsided, I knew one thing for certain. We were sure as hell going to find out.

I picked up the phone, pressing zero for an outside line. "Nothing," I said, hearing the long drone of a dead phone line. "No way to call out."

"We need to get downstairs and out of the building if we are going to make any sense of this," declared the big fella.

"Yeah, we do," I replied. "Only, the thing is, we don't know who's behind this, or if they're still here."

"But we've got to make contact with someone in authority. We can't deal with this alone."

"Too damn right," I replied.

I led the way out of the suite, past the dead Secret Service people, toward the elevator. We needed to call in the troops, but for the life of me, I couldn't figure out whose troops they should be.

Chapter 2

Seventy-Two Hours Earlier

Although a formal occasion, the crowd that packed the ball-room of the Al Gasr Hotel in downtown Khartoum were letting their hair down. People swayed and danced in time to the pumping music. I knew it was pumping because I was playing it. I leaned forward and ripped into a solo on the Hammond B3 organ. A rotating Leslie speaker converted the organ sound from a playful puppy into a howling wolf. It was the staple keyboard sound for any rhythm and blues band, and that's what we played: classic American rhythm and blues.

As I finished my solo, P.D. Bailey strolled casually up to the microphone. For a man in his late seventies, he played and sang with the energy of a twenty-year-old. The old bluesman had been around forever. He'd performed with Muddy Waters and B.B. King, sharing more joy and more pain in a lifetime of the blues than I could even imagine. P.D. Bailey: an American icon. It was an honor to share a stage with him.

I knew the other players in the band felt the same. As I watched Brian Pitt on drums, and Barry Flannigan on bass; they seemed to morph together as one driving, pulsing, rhythmical beast. I'd played with them both before; they were fantastic, inspiring musicians in their own rights, and yet their combined power on this stage, with P.D., ascended to a new level of ferocity.

The room was bedazzled in an assortment of color. Conservatively dressed Westerners faded into the background against the bright, lurid shades and patterns worn by our African hosts.

The fact that we were even here indicated a miracle in itself. Over the last twelve months, Sudan had evolved from a land burdened with internal conflict to a county with an increasingly stable democratic government. To ensure his position, and silence the nay-sayers, the new Sudanese president had opened up his country to the benefit of trade and cultural exchange with the outside world. His aim: to highlight the dynamism of democracy in the eyes of his people.

We were part of a political and artistic exposition that had brought powerful politicians, successful business people, and a variety of talented performers from across the world to Khartoum. From the Sudanese government's perspective, this was to be a tear-the-walls-down moment.

Standing on the stage, I could see the Sudanese president chatting amiably with the head of the American delegation, Vice President Jefferson Blake. The towering VP loomed over his African counterpart, their eyes locked in warm engagement. Skeptics had suggested Blake's leadership of the US team to be a contrived stunt; they professed that he was only here due to his African American heritage. But Blake hadn't been VP for long so hadn't had much of a chance to prove himself; he'd been seconded to the position when his predecessor became embroiled in a serious financial scandal. Jefferson Blake wasn't a career politician and was therefore untarnished in the eyes of the American public. Besides that, his outstanding military record had only added to his credibility.

Either way, as I watched them laughing together, it was obvious that our new vice president and Sudan's leader seemed to be getting along well. That had to be positive for both countries.

We'd flown in the day before. The vice president and his entourage had landed sometime after us on board Air Force Two. The Sudanese government had put on an impressive show to welcome them—I'd seen it on television. Our band had arrived earlier on a privately secured A-330, along with a variety of other musicians, business types, and diplomats, to considerably less fanfare. As our plane descended, the iridescent morning light had flooded Sudan's flat, arid landscape with subtle hues and deep shadows. I've seen my fair share of desert landscapes in the Middle East in times of conflict. I liked this one better.

Descending the stairs of our plane, the searing African heat had wrapped around us like a warm, restrictive blanket. Our feet had barely touched the scorching tarmac, when an excited-looking Sudanese man came bounding over. He looked to be in his mid-thirties and was dressed in neat, casual Western clothes. His eager face and ferocious smile did more for international public relations than a thousand welcoming speeches. The man held a sign. It read: P.D. Bailey and entourage. The smiling Sudanese seemed to recognize P.D. and called out, "*marhaba*, Welcome, Mr. Bailey, sir."

He then walked up to P.D., and shook his hand vigorously before waving us all over to a waiting minibus. As we climbed on board, the coolness of its air conditioning provided a genial sanctuary from the blazing heat. I sat next to Jack Greatrex. Jack had come along to look after our gear and do our sound.

"Well, here we go," I announced.

"It's nice to be here just for the music," he said.

I couldn't have agreed with him more. Recently we'd had enough 'extra-curricular activity' to last us a lifetime.

Our new host stood at the front of the bus and introduced himself as Jumaa Al Fadil.

"I am excited to welcome you all to Khartoum," he announced in unfaltering English. "This is a significant time for our country, and it is an honor to share our culture and our famous Sudanese hospitality with you. It is equally an honor to have the great P.D. Bailey and his band of talented musicians perform here. We now travel to the Al Saddaga resort where I'm sure you will be most comfortable and most secure. Vice President Blake and his entourage are also staying at this hotel. The staff there will be on hand for any requests or needs you may have.

Speech over, Jumaa Al Fadil bowed and offered us a cheeky grin. You had to like this guy.

An hour later, ensconced in our new luxury accommodation, Jack Greatrex and I shared a quiet Scotch as we lounged comfortably on the balcony of my room. We had invited Jumaa to join us. He accepted our invitation but declined to sit or to drink any alcohol. He stood with a Coke in his hand, leaning on the iron railing.

We eyed the sprawl of the growing metropolis. Like so many developing cities, Khartoum was a mixture of traditional brown earth-and-stone buildings combined with some exam-

9

ples of powerful modern architecture—new money. In the distance, we noticed two particularly distinctive and majestic-looking structures.

"What are they?" asked Greatrex, gesturing.

As Jumaa leaned over the railing, he waved toward the horizon and declared, "The structure on the right is the old presidential palace. The British built it during their time of, er... great influence. You can see that from its architectural styling."

"What about the building on the left?" I asked.

"Oh, that is the new presidential palace," said Jumaa. "That was constructed by the Chinese and opened in 2015."

"The Chinese?" I questioned.

"Yes, the Chinese worked closely with our former president, Omar al-Bashir."

Jumaa paused for a few seconds and then continued. "Fun fact—they opened the new palace exactly one hundred and thirty years to the day after the British governor of Khartoum was beheaded on the steps of the old palace."

"There's some food for thought," I said. "I guess they call that 'Concrete Diplomacy'."

"I think they call it sending a message," responded Greatrex. My friend paused a moment and then added, "Oh well, thank God we're here for the best of reasons. No beheadings on our agenda."

In silence, we sat there taking in the vast and varied view. I thought about the shows ahead of us, the chance to perform with the great P.D. Bailey and the company we were keeping. Where else would you want to be?

Forty-Eight Hours Earlier

The young girl at the reception desk smiled warmly as I inquired about her recommendation for a good local restaurant. Before she could respond, an assertive voice behind me interrupted.

"Mr. Sharp? Mr. Nicholas Sharp?"

I turned around to see a man the size of a small mountain dressed in a somber gray suit. He had an earpiece embedded in his right ear and from the bulge in his coat it was clear that he carried a weapon. I wasn't alarmed. He may as well have been wearing a sign that said, *I'm with the US Secret Service*.

"Yes," I responded.

"Mr. Sharp, I have an inquiry from Vice President Blake."

Unexpected.

"Yes?" I responded again.

"Sir, the vice president heard your name last night as they introduced the band. He says it rang a bell in the back of his mind. He wondered if by any chance you are related to Colonel Brighton Sharp of the US Marines?"

"Yes, I am," I replied. "He was my father."

"Respectfully, sir, if that's the case, I'm instructed to invite you up to the vice president's suite at three this afternoon. It would appear, sir, that Vice President Blake knew your father quite well."

I was taken aback. It's not every day that you get invited for a personal chat with the second most powerful man on earth.

There wasn't much I could say apart from, "I'll be there."

At 2.55 p.m., two poker-faced Secret Service agents escorted me out of the lift and onto the tenth-floor corridor. As we walked along the hallway, I sensed their professional appraisal, their X-ray eyes scanning me as a potential threat.

At the doorway to the vice president's suite, four more agents hovered.

"Mr. Sharp," said the elder and probably most senior of the group. He used a wand to scan me for personal weapons before knocking on the door. Without waiting for a response, he opened it and walked through. I followed him in. Another agent followed me.

It was an impressive and incontestably luxurious environment that I entered. The imposing figure standing in the center of the room was equally impressive. At close quarters, Vice President Jefferson Blake was a striking man. Marginally over six foot, evidently muscular, even under his well-cut business suit, he radiated a strength of character the most politicians would kill for.

"Mr. Sharp, Nicholas, if I may, please come in and sit down."

I took several steps toward him and held out my hand. "Mr. Vice President, it is an honor."

We both sat down.

"I'm sorry to drag you up here," he began, "but the Secret Service people seem to take exception to me prowling the corridors of hotels in foreign countries. It limits my movements."

"I understand, sir, not a problem." *Like I have anything else to do.* I continued. "I believe you knew my father?"

"Yes, I certainly did. He was a very influential person in my early military career. If it wasn't for him, I may well have walked a completely different road."

"How so, sir?" I asked.

"At one point I had doubts about staying in the Marines and pressing ahead with my military vocation. I was considering leaving to pursue a civil law career, focusing on social justice. Your father was the one person who made me see that the qualities and skills that I would pick up in the Marines would stay with me for life, even when I pursued other paths. Of course, he was right. I owe him a lot."

"He was very persuasive, and annoyingly logical in his arguments," I said. "I fear he had a similar impact on my own career choices."

"Were you a military man before you became a musician?"

"Yes, sir, a Marine scout sniper, three tours of duty."

"But you got out?"

"Yes, sir — I felt another calling." I saw no need to elaborate on what had been a complex situation, seeded in the back streets of Baghdad.

"It appears we may have a fair amount in common, Nicholas."

"Yes, sir, it does. Could I ask how you associated me with my father when you heard my name on stage last night?"

"Yes, I seemed to recall that at some point your father had mentioned you to me in passing conversation. He said that you had become an outstanding musician and a terrific shot with a rifle. He seemed uncertain which way you would fall."

That surprised me. My father never seemed uncertain about anything.

My leg started to vibrate followed by the distinctive sounds of my ringtone. *Shit.* I hadn't even left it on silent.

"I'm so sorry, sir—I must have forgotten to turn it off."

"Not a problem," said the vice president. I'll pour us each a drink while you take the call.

It was Greatrex.

"I can't talk now," I whispered. "I'm meeting with the vice president."

"Yeah, and I'm in a group chat with the Queen of England."

Some people believe nothing you say. I hung up.

13

Jefferson Blake and I spent the next twenty minutes chatting about life in the military and the exploits of my father, before being interrupted by one of his aides.

"I'm afraid I must send you on your way, Nicholas. Duty calls."

"Certainly, sir, it's been a pleasure."

"It surely has, my friend."

My friend.

A Secret Service agent seemed to appear out of nowhere to guide me to the door. I shook the vice president's hand and turned to follow the agent out.

Then, out of the blue, Jefferson Blake asked, "When do you fly out?"

"Tomorrow evening, after a final show with some local musicians," I responded.

With a chuckle, the vice president of the United States then made me an unrefusable offer. "We're flying out the morning after. How would you like a lift? If the press and my aides leave me alone long enough, we may get a chance to exchange some more Brighton Sharp stories."

"Thank you, Mr. Vice President, that would be an honor." I paused for a moment. "Sir, without being presumptuous, is there any chance I can bring a colleague along? He's also a former Marine now working in the music industry."

Blake looked undecided, but only for a second. "Sure thing, why not?"

I turned and left the room.

So, Greatrex and I were going for a ride on Air Force Two. Who would have thought?

Chapter 3

Now

The lobby was still eerily silent. Fortunately, no surprises there.

Greatrex and I traversed the vast space, searching for any sign of life as we walked. We saw no one, just an empty cavernous expanse that seemed all wrong. When we passed an impressively sizable indoor atrium and happened into sight of the large glass front doors, everything changed. Several men in khaki military fatigues blocked the hotel entrance. They seemed tense and alert but faced away from us toward the street outside.

As we approached the doors, they automatically opened. The soldiers seemed to be surprised at the sound and quickly swung around. When they swiveled, they instinctively raised their weapons. Jack Greatrex and I found ourselves staring down the barrels of six high-powered rifles.

"Hey, calm down, fellas," I suggested as we both raised our arms. "We don't want any accidents."

One of the soldiers, the first to regain his composure, stepped forward. By the epaulets on his shoulders, I assumed him to be the most senior ranking officer.

"Who are you?" he demanded in faltering English.

"Nicholas Sharp and Jack Greatrex. We are musicians with the US exposition contingent," I said. "Officer, something is dreadfully wrong. There are—"

Before I could finish, the officer interrupted. "All the performers and extra US personnel flew out at midnight last night. How can I be sure you are who you say you are and why are you still here?" Before I could reply he continued aggressively. "Identification papers and passports, please. Now!"

"They are up in our rooms," replied Greatrex. "You need to listen to us…"

The Sudanese officer looked decidedly uncomfortable. He had made no comment regarding the empty hotel, and he seemed quite perturbed to see us.

"One moment," he said.

The soldier sidled a few paces aside, out of earshot, and whispered hurriedly into his radio. A couple of minutes later he returned. He didn't look happy.

"You are to go back inside and wait in the hotel lobby. Two of my men will accompany you. My commanding officer will be here shortly."

He spoke to the two men nearest him in rapid Arabic. On cue, they indicated toward the empty lobby with their rifles before unceremoniously marching us back through the glass doors and into the hotel.

"Tell me I'm dreaming," I said to Greatrex.

"'Fraid not," replied the big fella. "That man didn't want to hear a word we had to say. It was like he already knew."

"*Agot tahit was as 'kut!*," barked one of the soldiers. Neither of us spoke the language, but he undoubtedly meant that we should sit down and shut up.

Twenty minutes later, a Sudanese Army SUV in camouflage livery pulled up in front of the hotel. A very official-looking soldier in an overly tidy uniform laced with braid and military ribbon bars stepped out. On the crown of his head, an olive-green beret featuring a red and gold insignia enforced his status. After talking briefly with the officer on duty, he marched through the lobby doors toward us.

"I am Colonel Agiid Abdulmuti Al Bahari Tijan of the Sudanese Armed Forces. Who might you be?" inquired the colonel in impeccable English.

Again, we identified ourselves.

"You were due to leave Khartoum last night. Why are you still here?" he demanded.

My frustration growing rapidly by the minute, I responded.

"Colonel, why we are still here is a long story and doesn't really matter. The point is, there are dead American Secret Service personnel scattered around this building. There is no one else in sight, and it appears that the vice president of the United States of America has gone missing."

The colonel said nothing. He stared at us as though we were aliens.

Finally, "We are aware of the situation."

"You are *aware*? Please tell us what the hell you are aware of? Nothing is making sense here." My patience abandoned me completely.

Again, the colonel waited before he answered.

"There is a situation. It has national and international ramifications. These events do not involve you."

"Of course they damn well involve us," said Greatrex. "We

are sitting right in the middle of the whole freakin' mess."

More silence.

Then, "You two gentlemen are to return to your rooms. Do not leave the hotel. Do not make any further explorations around the hotel. I will have men stationed on your floor. All remaining guests have been evacuated. We will make the same arrangements for you shortly."

"With respect, Colonel, that is nowhere near good enough. We insist that you make provisions for us to be taken to the US Embassy immediately," I demanded.

"That will not happen, Mr. Sharp. Your embassy has been... isolated. No one is entering nor leaving it. All electronic communication to and from the embassy has also been blocked."

Greatrex and I glanced at each other. *What the...?*

Too much was unclear, but evidently we had landed ourselves in some kind of major political upheaval. The situation ran so far above our pay grade it was ridiculous.

"Colonel, can you at least tell us the status and location of Vice President Jefferson Blake?" I requested.

"I'm afraid that information is not available to me, nor to you. Now, gentlemen, my men will escort you to your rooms. Good afternoon." With that, Colonel Agiid Abdulmuti Al Bahari Tijan turned around and left.

"Just here for the music?" I said, looking at Greatrex.

"No comment," came the terse reply.

Greatrex was sitting in a lounge chair; I was perched on the end of the bed in my room. The soldiers hadn't insisted we go to our separate rooms as we both had accommodation on the same floor. Guarding one room equated to an easier task.

"This feels so far beyond 'not right' that it's absurd," I said.

"It makes no sense," observed the big fella. "Getting caught up in a political coup in a reasonably unstable country is one thing. When American personnel are killed and a sitting US vice president goes AWOL, well, that's a whole different level of nightmare."

"We need to find a way to communicate with US authorities. We have no idea how much they know about what's going on here. I can't imagine anyone in Washington is twiddling their thumbs while the second-in-command of the county has gone 'location status unknown,'" I replied.

I pulled out my cell phone for what must have been the tenth time. Still no signal. We had also tried my laptop. The toolbar at the bottom of the screen indicated no internet connection.

"Short of smoke signals, I have no ideas," I concluded.

Abruptly there was a knock on the door.

"Come in, it's open," ordered Greatrex.

To our surprise, in strolled Jumaa Al Fadil, our guide from a few days ago. He carried a tray of food.

"How in God's name…?" I began.

"A few piasters here, a few American dollars there, and I managed to persuade the soldiers guarding the hotel that you would need food. No one wanted to be responsible for your malnourishment," he laughed.

"How did you know we were here?" asked Greatrex.

"Quite straightforward really," said Jumaa. "Remember, I remained with you last night until well after the plane with most of your contingent left? When I heard of the unrest, I came straight to the hotel, knowing that you would not have made it out of the country with your fellow countrymen. I saw the soldiers loading a few remaining guests into a bus,

19

presumably to be taken to the airport for another flight out."

"And we weren't among the guests," I added.

"No, I figured the soldiers wouldn't have checked your rooms because they assumed you left last night. No one suspected you had arranged to catch a lift with the vice president. I tried to tell the soldiers, but no one wanted to listen."

"You are a very resourceful man, Jumaa," said Greatrex.

"I'm beginning to think we don't appreciate the half of it," I chipped in.

Jumaa just offered his sassy grin and shrugged.

"Well, my inventive friend, you better tell us what you know. We are flying blind here, and obviously something has gone terribly wrong." I sat and waited.

Jumaa began, "Yes, in the middle of the night there was an uprising, a coup. As you are aware, those in charge of the military here have been struggling in a leadership battle for some years with those promoting democratic reform. We hoped we had made it through that period, but... apparently not."

Our Sudanese friend paused thoughtfully for a moment before continuing.

"I suspect that the success of the international exposition of which you are a part, in addition to the very positive relationship that has developed between our president and your vice president, has played a role in this."

"How so?" asked Greatrex.

"Well, there are some in the military and many others in extreme Islamic groups that believe that the movement for democratic change is not right for our county. They are convinced it will have a negative impact on our people's religious rights. They see Christianity as a threat, and the intrusion of the West represents that threat. Accordingly, the success of the exposition had become an overwhelming problem for those opposing democracy."

I marveled at Jumaa's succinct appraisal of Sudanese politics.

"You are a bit more than just a tour guide, aren't you, Jumaa?" I suggested.

"Yes, perhaps. I have been quite active in the movement for constitutional change. I have also been very fortunate to avoid the wrath of those who oppose it," he replied.

"Okay," said Greatrex. "I get the whole thing about the continuing instability, but surely kidnapping a US vice president and murdering Secret Service agents couldn't be part of a bigger plan for the country's management?"

"Yes, I'm sure you are right," responded Jumaa. "As we speak, I have no doubt that our country's military and civilian leaders are negotiating their way through this situation. They have done it many times before. The trouble is, many of our religious zealots have seen this as well and are growing tired of the dance. I'm fairly certain that the deaths of your countrymen and the removal of Vice President Jefferson Blake have been actioned by an outlying radical extremist group."

"You mean terrorists," I said.

"Yes, Nicholas. I don't want to alarm you, but it is my belief that Vice President Blake has been kidnapped. It is also my belief that the most likely group responsible are violent Islamic terrorists from within my country."

Neither Greatrex nor I responded.

"One more thing," added Jumaa, "if these people are part of or in any way related to the extremist group I am thinking of..." Our new friend seemed to hesitate.

21

"Well?" I asked

"Well, they will not hesitate to kill your man if they don't get what they want."

Chapter 4

The three of us sat in silence.

It wasn't my nature, nor I'm sure anyone else's in that room, to let this go and just wait to be safely rescued. That is, of course, if that's what the authorities had planned for us. I knew we would try to do something, but I had no idea what.

"Communication," announced Greatrex, "that has to be the first step. We can't do anything until we get in touch with the US government. We don't know if they are planning something as we speak. If we get in their way, we could be creating more problems."

"On the other hand, if they don't know what's happened, they won't be planning anything and we'll need to act," I added. "Jumaa, how much information about all of this has gotten out of the country?"

"I'm sure the world knows there has been some sort of coup. They wouldn't have let people fly out if secrecy had been their main concern. I'm equally sure your president will be worried—he should be. The trouble is that the Sudanese authorities are very good at controlling the flow of information across our borders. While it's probably public knowledge that there has been unrest, the details will be sketchy. Those in power have shut down the internet and blocked any electronic communications. The embassies in Khartoum would have been the first locations they targeted."

"Then it's likely that our people have no idea that the vice president has been kidnapped by terrorists," I observed.

"Yes, Nicholas, it is most unlikely that they will be aware of that," said Jumaa.

"As I said, communication," said Greatrex. "But how?"

The room reverted to a frustrated silence.

Several minutes later, I said, "I have an idea. It's the original longshot, but there may be a chance."

"Pray continue, oh enlightened one," said the big fella.

"Well," I began, "restricting online networks is relatively straightforward for a government. We've seen that many times before. On the other hand, blocking electronic communications beyond the cell-phone level requires strategic targeting. They've blocked the embassies and they've blocked this hotel because the vice president's team would have had a strong comms set-up in place."

"Go on," said Greatrex.

"Where else would we find such a powerful communications set-up in Khartoum?"

No reply.

"If it hasn't been destroyed or blocked by the terrorists, it will be sitting at the Khartoum International Airport," I said.

Greatrex smiled.

Jumaa looked perplexed.

"Yes, I'm talking about the vice president's ride: Air Force Two."

The three of us sat on the front seat of Jumaa's aging white Toyota Land Cruiser. The streets of Khartoum appeared

24

quiet. A dusty silence hung over the city, dampening its usual vibrance. I wondered if the country's political unrest had become so routine that the move to 'shutdown' when there was upheaval was positively habitual.

Jumaa's plan to get us out of the hotel showed brilliance in its simplicity. He had brought enough food into the hotel to feed a small army, so that's exactly what he did. After setting up a table overflowing with food at one end of the corridor outside our room, he invited the guards to feast. They obliged. Having strategically set up two comfortable chairs facing the small table of food but away from the direction of our rooms, Jumaa ensured that the guards' attention remained distracted.

While the guards ate, Greatrex and I slipped quietly along the corridor and into the stairwell. The downward journey turned into a long, spiraling trek as we did our best to mute the loud echo of our footsteps. We padded down the treads as silently as possible. When we reached the bottom, Jumaa was waiting. Our guide knew his way around the hotel and after following him through a series of corridors and the expansive commercial kitchen, we arrived outside before we knew it. And parked right in front of the door was Jumaa's Land Cruiser; it was as though he had planned all this ahead of time. The more I got to know this man, the more I realized there was no end to his resourcefulness.

"If we are stopped by anyone, let me do the talking," Jumaa had instructed. "There are enough Westerners in this city that we can explain you away as airport maintenance staff being called in to work at the airport. It won't fool anyone for an extended period but should give us enough time to do what we need to do."

Greatrex and I didn't argue.

Feeling very exposed as we drove along one near-deserted street after another, I sensed relief when Jumaa finally announced, "We are almost there."

As we turned off the appropriately named Africa Street, an array of army vehicles parked up near the arches of the terminal complex came into view. The military had evidently taken over the airport.

"Surely this is going to be too difficult," I said. "If the army is everywhere, we'll never get to the plane."

Jumaa then veered right.

"This is the VIP section of the airport. It is most likely that your vice president's plane will be in this area."

He stopped the car outside a large industrial-looking building, its bland corrugated-iron walls towering above us as we climbed out. Apart from the intense midafternoon heat, the first thing that hit me was the lack of soldiers within sight in this part of the complex.

"This is strange," said our guide as we walked past a series of maintenance related buildings. "I would have expected to be stopped and questioned by now."

"There's no way the army would have just ignored the VIP section of the terminal?" I asked.

"Not a chance — the army is experienced in closing down this facility. It has happened many times before, but not usually when the United States' vice president's plane is here."

I nodded.

"This just doesn't seem right," Jumaa added.

We turned another corner and found ourselves standing at the edge of an expansive section of tarmac. Two high-end private jets stood idle, glistening in the sun. Neither one was Air Force Two. On the far side of the tarmac, another oversized hangar dominated the skyline.

"We will try in there," said Jumaa.

Three minutes later, our luck ran out again. The hangar was empty.

"Follow me," said our guide.

As we rounded the building on its east side, another hangar appeared before us. Its enormous bulk suggested it was big enough to hold a commercial jet, but its closed doors blocked any view inside. As we stepped forward, all eyes on the hangar, we virtually tripped over the motionless body of a Sudanese soldier lying on the ground. He lay at an awkward, unnatural angle. Blood seeped out of a bullet wound in his head, suggesting he'd been alive only minutes ago. Now he was clearly dead.

"Crap," said the ever-observant Jack Greatrex.

"This is not good," said Jumaa. "I'm thinking the army does not have control of this area of the airport."

I was about to ask, 'Then who the hell does?' when the first round of bullets echoed in a machine-like thunder across the tarmac, penetrating the tin wall just above our heads.

"Down," I yelled. Nicholas Sharp: stating the obvious.

The three of us hit the ground, clumsily struggling as we crawled our way back around the corner.

More bullets kicked up a trail of chipped concrete in front of us as we retreated.

"I'm betting the vice president's plane is inside that hangar," I said. "We need to find a way in."

"I'll double back around and try for a rear entrance," said Greatrex.

"We are unarmed, and they have guns," observed Jumaa. He looked surprised but not frightened.

"Hold that thought," I said.

Before anyone argued with me, I leaped around the corner and dove down beside the dead soldier. My hands reeled as the radiant heat of the tarmac burned my skin. As if on cue, another round of gunfire echoed loudly above my head. I reached over the lifeless body and frantically wrestled the soldier's Helcher & Koch G3 rifle from his hands before taking aim and returning fire in the general direction of our attacker. Using my own fire as cover, I got up and sprinted back around the corner of the hangar to join the others.

"Well, now we have a gun," I announced.

Jumaa just stared at me, a look of disbelief on his face.

"Don't ask," said Greatrex, no further conversation.

I gave Greatrex five minutes to find his way around the back of the building before I leaned cautiously around the corner and fired off a few more rounds.

"You wait here," I said to Jumaa as I took off across the tarmac, the wheels of the closest plane offering the only protection in sight. More gunfire erupted, but zigzagging made me a difficult target. When I made it to the plane, I noticed that the sniper had located himself behind the side door of the hangar, still some distance away. It takes one to find one.

Greatrex had better come through. I moved off, launching myself toward the wheels of the next parked plane a good eighty feet away — it felt more like eighty miles when the sniper opened up again.

I'd almost made it when suddenly a stream of bullets hit the tarmac directly in front of my running feet. Then the same thing happened directly behind me, shards of concrete spraying everywhere. With nowhere to go, I became imprisoned by the gunfire. In one brief instant, the situation had become irretrievable.

I dove to the ground as I waited for the next hail of bullets to tear through my skin.

Then the gunfire stopped. I raised my head to see Greatrex standing at the side door where my would-be sniper had been. I saw a body lying at his feet. I didn't hesitate. Back on my feet, I ran like all hell in his direction.

"I figured I was done," I said as I took cover behind the office door next to the big fella.

"While he fired at you, I managed to get the drop on him," said Greatrex, indicating in the direction of the fallen gunman.

"Next time you be the target," I chuckled, amused but maybe also a little serious.

I looked at the dead man lying at our feet. He wore a long, white, loose-fitting collarless, and now bloodied robe. A galabiya. A similarly white skullcap clung tightly to his head. Typical Northern Sudanese clothing. But the most important takeaway was that his attire was not military uniform. While Greatrex took his gun, I searched him for identification. He carried none.

"He's obviously not with the SAF," I said.

"I'm thinking perhaps the breakaway Islamic terrorist group that Jumaa told us about," said the big fella.

"That means he will probably have some friends around here somewhere."

"After that volume of gunfire, the SAF soldiers at the main terminal will most likely be on their way here as we speak. We don't have much time before this place becomes a hellhole of destruction," he said.

Without saying more, we both turned and stepped through

the hangar door into a small office area. At least now we both had weapons, which gave us—literally—a fighting chance.

There was no one in the room, but two doors led off the area. I indicated for Greatrex to take the door on the left while I moved right. Before I even got to my allocated door, Greatrex had his open.

"Damn and shit," he exclaimed as he waved me over.

"Damn and shit indeed," I said as I stepped toward him and look over his shoulder into the small room.

A pile of dead bodies lay haphazardly across the small room. Some wore SAF uniforms, some wore the distinctive dark suits of the Secret Service, and a couple were dressed in US Air Force uniforms. I presumed these to be the pilots of the vice president's plane.

"In case we had any doubts," I said, "these bastards are playing for keeps."

The bile rose in my throat, but I saw no point standing there mourning the loss of life. We needed to move, and quickly. Both Greatrex and I had been trained to partition our emotions under pressure. Soldiers are good at building emotional walls, but not so good at tearing them down.

As we strode toward the other doorway, the big fella stopped and turned to me.

"Why are the terrorists here?" he asked. "I assumed they'd be as far away from Khartoum as possible by now."

"I've been thinking about that since the first round of gunfire," I responded. "The only thing that makes sense to me is that they came here for the same reason we did. I reckon they want to use the comms center on Air Force Two as a way to directly notify the authorities in the States that they have Vice President Blake."

Greatrex nodded.

We reached the next door.

"On my count," I said. "One, two, three."

Greatrex pulled the door open with one hand while holding up his newly acquired weapon in the other. I went low and moved through the doorway with my rifle, scanning the area. To my relief, there was no barrage of gunfire to greet us. Then I wondered why.

The gigantic hangar stood silent. Once we realized we were safe—for now—our attention focused on the gleaming Boeing C-32 sitting in the center of the space. The gleaming white-and-blue coloring at once recognizable as the vice president's plane, Air Force Two.

We stayed in the doorway for a few seconds, effecting a visual reconnaissance of the large space. We saw no one. It occurred to me that if the terrorists had been and gone, why did they leave a man guarding the building? Eventually the penny dropped.

"I'd put money on the fact that they are inside the plane and didn't hear the gunfire outside," I said.

"VIP aircraft can be well soundproofed," said Greatrex. "It makes sense."

"Okay," I said. "Decision time. Do we move forward and confront these bastards, even though we don't know how many people are aboard, or do we beat a hasty retreat? There will be other ways to make contact stateside."

We looked at each other.

"There's no choice to be made here," said Greatrex. "Getting one of these people to talk may be our only way of finding out where the VP is being held. Besides, we need to make contact with the outside world now."

Damn his patriotic logic.

"All right," I said. "Forward it is."

We split up. Jack made his way toward the rear of the aircraft, using the aviation equipment scattered around the hanger as cover. I did the same, heading toward the nose of the plane.

We met at the stairs on the far side of the aircraft; the only way in.

"This may get ugly," said the big fella.

"Let's go," I said. "If we make it to the top of the stairs, you go aft, I'll go forward."

With that, we silently climbed the stairway.

Air Force Two is not laid out like a normal passenger plane. As we peeked into the entrance way, we could see a corridor leading to a larger cabin at the back. I reasoned the comms set-up would to be toward the front, near the cockpit, so I headed that way. If a firefight ensued in this enclosed space, I figured that greater numbers wouldn't necessarily be a big advantage for the terrorists. At least that's what I told myself as I stole forward.

I made it almost halfway up the corridor when a toilet door on my right suddenly opened. I had nowhere to go. A large man, also wearing the traditional galabiya, stepped in front of me. He saw me straightaway. Fortunately, I'd had a second's warning. He had none.

The man began to reach into his robes, I quickly reversed my rifle, raised it and shoved the butt into the side of his head with as much force as I could muster in the confined space. He staggered sideways, clearly stunned. Before he responded further, I swung the butt again, an upward motion hard into his chin. He crumpled. He was unconscious before he hit the floor.

Greatrex had heard the noise and appeared behind me. I reached down to see what my opponent had been struggling to reach for under his robes. I pulled out a large khanjar, a fierce enough knife to take my head off with a single swipe. Thank God the man hadn't got to it in time.

"Let's work as a unit rather than separate," whispered Greatrex.

I nodded.

We crept silently up the corridor before coming to a closed door at the far end. We heard voices coming from the other side; Arabic, and the tone sounded agitated. I didn't understand the words, but it was obvious several people occupied the room ahead of us.

"This is it," I said. "We go in together, firing. If there's room, I'll go right, you go left. If there's no room you go low, I'll go high. Try not to shoot me."

My calm exterior belied the seriousness of the situation we prepared to face.

"One, two, three!"

After Greatrex turned the handle, I kicked the door open.

It took me less than a second to realize that we were totally outgunned. At least six men in the room, with most of them clutching Kalashnikov assault rifles tightly in their hands. The two who didn't hold guns huddled over a complicated-looking communications system, their rifles lying on the bench next to them.

We had no choice but to fire quickly and decisively. I took out the two men on the right. Double taps into each of their chests. As discussed, Greatrex fired left. It was like a scene out of *Pulp Fiction*; noise and blood assaulting the senses, men yelling, screaming… and dying.

A man at the far end of the room reacted quickly and got a shot off. Taller than the others, slightly further away, he was clearly more focused. Fortunately, I had pushed forward and to my right after my opening barrage and his shot went wide. Before he managed another shot, Greatrex took him out with a short burst straight into his face. The bloodied corpse collapsed in a crippled heap.

Greatrex had the automatic weapon. He fired at the man sitting at the desk. The first rounds virtually took his arms off as the target died in a pool of blood and metal. The whole firefight took less than ten seconds. The last terrorist remained sitting at the comms desk, his hands on the surface in front of him. He looked at us without moving. His eyes kept darting to the Kalashnikov sitting about a foot to his right.

"I wouldn't," said Greatrex.

The man probably didn't understand the language, but he appeared to understand the meaning of Greatrex's tone. His shoulders seemed to slump in resignation. Then suddenly he leaped to his feet, yelled something we didn't understand and threw himself toward his weapon. He died before his fingers touched the gun.

"That didn't need to happen," said Greatrex, who had just fired the shot. "It was pointless."

"Just think about those dead bodies in that room back there," I nodded in the direction of the office. "I wouldn't call it pointless — more like justice," I said.

"And justice is what you will face," said a sullen voice behind us. "Weapons on the ground... Now!"

Greatrex and I turned our heads around slowly. We didn't want to make any movement that could be misunderstood. A tall, dark figure stood in the doorway. He was breathing hard, but his hands were steady. They were holding a Kalashnikov. The gun swept a lethal arc between Greatrex and me. We put our guns on the carpet. As if we had a choice.

"You have caused an unexpected and needless delay to our task," he began. His voice resonated in a deep, calm tone, his English accented, but faultless. His simmering anger appeared to build like an approaching tempest as he surveyed the damage we had caused. "I don't know who you infidels are, nor do I care. I see you have murdered several of my brothers. That was undeserved, although they will be accepted into Paradise as they died carrying out God's glorious work."

The man paused. His eyes showed a flicker of watery sadness before the corners of his mouth turned downward and his forehead creased.

"If you have a God, I suggest you make peace with him now because you are about to meet him face to face." The terrorist's dark features furrowed even further as he began to squeeze the trigger. His gun was now pointed solely at me. For the second time today, I saw no way out.

The next half-second seemed like an eternity. I glanced at Greatrex. The horror and frustration in his wide eyes told the story. I took a breath, assuming it to be my last.

Suddenly my would-be executioner let out an anguished cry and fell forward, sprawling at our feet on the cabin floor. I saw why. The khanjar that I had stupidly left on the unconscious terrorist in the hallway protruded from the center of his back. A waterfall of deep-red blood streamed from the wound.

Feeling the relief of a man who has just escaped a death sentence, I looked up to see a grinning Jumaa gazing around the room.

"It is just as well I have trouble following instructions," he said.

He was inordinately calm for someone who wasn't a combat professional but had just taken a life.

I sensed a smile slink onto my face as I said, "As mentioned earlier, Jumaa, I think there is more to you than meets the eye."

Our Sudanese friend just tilted his head to one side and grinned.

Chapter 5

"I think we better get out of here quickly," said Jumaa. "The SAF troops will have heard the gunfire from outside and be on their way."

I looked around the cabin. The communications equipment was now a bloodied mess with a few more holes in it now than the engineers intended. It wasn't designed to be at the center of a firefight.

"Well, any chance of using this gear is gone," I said. "On the good side, we're still alive, so let's make the most of it and disappear."

The big fella nodded.

"Although before we go, I think we should take a second to question our friend in the corridor, if he's conscious. He may give us some idea about where they are holding Blake," I continued.

"It's worth a shot," said Greatrex.

It wasn't. The remaining live terrorist remained dead to the world.

"Bring him with us," I instructed. "I want to be there when he comes to."

Jumaa looked worried. "If we are stopped by the army with an unconscious man in the truck, it will raise suspicions. It would be very hard to explain."

"It's worth the risk," said Greatrex. "He may be our only lead."

With that, the big fella heaved the limp body up over his shoulder and we descended the aircraft steps.

We'd just made it back to Jumaa's Land Cruiser when we heard the screech of tires and voices yelling coming from the hangar.

Greatrex threw the unconscious terrorist on the back seat and climbed in next to him. Jumaa and I got in the front.

"Let's move it," I said. Jumaa responded by flooring the gas pedal.

The fading light cast long shadows as we drove through the streets of Khartoum. There seemed a little more traffic around now. It appeared people had overcome their initial shock at another moment of political unrest and resumed their lives.

"I have a place in Al-Lamap," said Jumaa. "It is very private, and not too far from here. The less time we spend on the streets with our guest, the better."

"All right," I responded. "We can come up with some sort of plan after we get there."

Jumaa didn't alter the direction of the vehicle. I had the feeling he had already decided that his home was the safest place to hole up.

As we turned westward onto a relatively major arterial road, a bank of traffic in front of us caused us to slow to a crawl before stopping.

"Military roadblock," announced Jumaa. "This could be difficult."

"Can we turn around?" asked Greatrex.

"That would invite inspection at the best, detention at the

worst," responded our host. "We must wait and see how the cards fall."

That kind of waiting was not my strong suit. I liked to have control. Sitting here, we had none.

"Pass me your gun," said Greatrex.

I'd held on to the dead SAF soldiers' rifle in case we needed it again. Greatrex had done the same with his Kalashnikov. As I passed my weapon over to him, he shoved them both on the floor of the back seat. He peeled some robes off our terrorist guest and covered the guns with it.

"Sit our friend upright," instructed Jumaa. "Let him lean against you."

Greatrex did as instructed.

As we waited in line, the late afternoon sun faded into twilight. More people, mostly men, gathered in groups along the wide sidewalks. Although difficult to tell from a distance, their animated body language suggested an element of tension in their conversations. As news of the coup spread, stories, both true and inaccurate, would emerge. Would the unrest build or subside? The streets of Khartoum had evolved into a bloody mess of violence several times before.

Ahead of us, military personnel in dusty green uniforms blocked the now floodlit street with army supply trucks. As we drew closer, it became obvious that the soldiers were heavily armed. No vehicle was getting through without being stopped and questioned.

We sat there in silence. As Jumaa had mentioned, it was too late to make a break for it, and any physical confrontation with this many troops could only end badly for us. Our immediate future lay in our new friend's ability to talk our way through this.

Finally, as we rolled to a halt at the front of the queue, armed SAF soldiers appeared on each side of the car. Jumaa wound down his window before being requested. Proactive.

A heated exchange of words became quickly strained. Greatrex and I understood none of what was said. At one point, the soldier questioning Jumaa indicated with his rifle to the comatose passenger in the back seat. The soldier raised his voice and repeated, "*Al zul de ghamran leh?*"

Jumaa appeared relaxed, although I had no doubt that he felt as tense as hell. He responded to the soldier while smiling and gesticulating from the driver's seat. At one point, he seemed to be pretending to take a drink.

The soldier paused. He took a good look at the man in the back seat next to Greatrex. Suddenly the soldier burst out laughing and animatedly kicked his foot high up in the air. After that, he waved us through.

We didn't speak for a good two minutes, not until we made it well clear of the roadblock.

"What the hell happened there?" I asked.

Jumaa quietly chuckled to himself. "You know, I really didn't think that would work," he announced.

"What did you tell them?" asked Greatrex.

"I said that you two worked with a Western maintenance crew employed by Boeing. I also said that our friend was your local liaison. I mentioned that being weak-willed Westerners, you'd both been unnerved about being caught up in a strange country in the middle of such unrest. I told him you downed a few drinks this afternoon to calm yourselves."

"How did you explain our unconscious companion?" I asked.

Jumaa grinned again. "I said that he had tried to keep up with you and also consumed some alcohol. I told them he was

Muslim and had broken sharia law. I said not only would his community at the local mosque be unhappy with him, but also his wife when I told her."

"What about the kick in the air?" asked the big fella.

"The soldier said that there could be no punishment he was able to inflict that could be worse than what his wife would do. That's when he moved us on."

Ten minutes later we pulled up in front of a small concrete-block building at the end of a narrow dirt road. A small veranda, with a painted railing and an old refrigerator sitting by the front door, ran the width of the house. Jumaa's home may not have been particularly upmarket, but it appeared well cared for.

Other buildings of a similar size but in a variety of conditions populated the surrounding area.

Our Sudanese guide pulled up with the back door of the Toyota adjacent to the front door of the shack. Although darkness had fallen, it didn't pay to bring unwanted attention to our visitor. Jumaa jumped out of the driver's seat, walked around the vehicle, and helped Greatrex carry the hostage inside.

I followed carrying the two guns, still wrapped in the man's robes.

The inside of the shack was as spartan as the outside. The dwelling consisted of two rooms: one for living and one for sleeping. Both rooms had hard stone floors. A small, cluttered kitchen area perched in shadow at one end of the tiny living room. Like the outside, the interior of the building looked neat and well cared for.

Greatrex and Jumaa dumped our prisoner onto an upright kitchen chair. Jumaa reached into a cupboard, produced some rope and proceeded to tie our man to his seat.

"You must have really clobbered him," observed Greatrex. "He's still totally out of it."

"I didn't have much choice at the time," I responded.

"Well," announced Jumaa. "I will provide some food while we come up with a plan, eh?"

"We still need to find a way of contacting the American authorities," I added. "That has to be a priority."

"I may be able to help with that," said Jumaa, a cooking pot already in his hand, "but first, we eat and wait."

In the right circumstances, a sniper's dominant skill is patience, along with an acute ability to observe. The addition of Jumaa's cooking was a bonus as we spent the next hour eating, planning, and waiting.

I knew that if we could get him to talk, whatever our captive terrorist had to say would have a large impact on the next twenty-four hours of our lives. I just hoped his words would also have a positive impact on the life of US Vice President Jefferson Blake.

Chapter 6

The groaning began around an hour later.

Over the following ten minutes, our captive gradually regained consciousness. It would be anyone's first instinct to show a recovering man a little sympathy, maybe offer him water. But as the terrorist became more lucid, I considered the dead men and women he had left in his wake. My mind went to the pile of corpses in the office at the airport and the Secret Service agents who perished at the hotel. I wondered what compassion our prisoner and his friends had shown them.

My animosity built to rage. When he pleaded for a drink, I slapped him hard across the face, out of character, but also out of patience. No water.

"Nicholas," said Greatrex, a firm agitation in his voice.

"I know, I know," I responded. "I'm just pissed."

Jumaa brought a jug of water over to our prisoner. He placed it on the floor, six inches beyond his reach.

"Motivation," he declared.

Greatrex walked behind the chair, reached down, grabbed the terrorist's hair and yanked him backward. I stared into the rebel's eyes. Bitter hatred. His and mine.

"I've killed many men," I began. Jumaa's eyes widened as I spoke. Astonishment, perhaps even alarm—clearly beginning to understand his guests were a little more experienced than he'd bargained for. "It will mean nothing to me to kill one more. Do you understand?"

The man tried to nod, but Greatrex's grip held him hard against the back of the chair.

"Tell me what I need, and you may survive," I demanded. No response.

Our prisoner's features crunched into a snarl. Through bared teeth, he spat. "My life has no importance. You and your infidel kind will burn in hell alongside all murderers of the innocent. My God is great."

Greatrex tightened his grip. The man's pain was palpable.

"Then I'll not waste my time," I replied.

I got up and strode over to the cupboard where the gun I had taken from the dead SAF soldier was leaning. I picked it up and released the safety. Pointing the weapon at the terrorist, I nodded in Jumaa's direction asking, "Will your neighbors react to the noise of a gunshot? I'll only need one."

"It is not a problem," he replied. "Gunfire is not unusual around here during times of unrest."

I studied the man on the chair. For a brief second, there was hesitation.

"Where is Vice President Jefferson Blake being held? You have ten seconds to decide if you live or die." I stepped closer to him. The rifle barrel was an inch from his cheek.

To my surprise, Jumaa took a pace forward, crouched down and whispered into our captive's ear. He spoke in Arabic. What was he doing? When he had finished, he pushed the jug toward the man then nodded, as if to prompt him.

The seconds ticked past. No one uttered a word. I felt my finger tightening on the trigger when the terrorist yelled,

"*Shararaa!*"

"What did you say?" I demanded.

Suddenly, without warning, Jumaa swept down, picked up the jug and smashed it over the terrorist's skull. Blood, water, and pottery sprayed across the room. What remained of the man's head rolled to one side. Life extinguished.

Greatrex looked surprised. I was furious.

"Why in God's name did you do that, Jumaa?" I yelled.

"He is my countryman," replied the Sudanese man. "It is only right that I am the one to inflict justice upon him." Anger.

"But he told us nothing. We needed his information." I tensed in frustration. "You've killed our only lead."

Silence.

"Nicholas," Jumaa began, "when I heard you speak to this zealot, I could feel your rage. Between the fervor you displayed at the airport, and your approach here tonight, I sensed that you and Jack have not been totally transparent with me—no civilian would ever be able to handle these weapons with such precision. I was also certain that you would not allow this man to survive. It was a simple choice. Does he die by your hand or mine?"

"But…" I began.

"What did you say to him?" interrupted Greatrex. "What did you say just before you used the jug as a flyswat?"

"I informed him that his God had presented him with two paths. He could either cooperate with us, and be rested and replenished, or deny us, and die within seconds. The jug of water was the symbol of our good faith."

Jumaa turned toward me, frowning. "I saw the answer in his eyes, Nicholas. He would never talk."

"So, we are nowhere," said Greatrex.

45

"No," continued our Sudanese friend, "my last words to this fool were 'you will die alone for nothing and you fight in no one's name.'"

Neither Greatrex nor I spoke. It was clear Jumna had more to say.

"In his anger, our deluded warrior made his stand, preparing to die in the name of his tribe." Jumaa looked Greatrex and I up and down, as though expecting a response.

Silence.

Jumaa permitted himself a slight grin. "I fear I've not been clear. When he cried out, *Shararaa*, I glimpsed into this man's evil soul. I saw his world and the deathly brothers with whom he walked. With one word he told us everything." The Sudanese shrugged his shoulders. "So I helped him along the journey down his God's pathway."

"And..." I waited.

"The information will be helpful, but... I'm afraid it is terrible news."

I sagged.

"First, you must realize what is happening here," began Jumaa. "I've told you of the continual conflict between the pro-democratic movement and those who believe that Sharia law should rule Sudan. This struggle seems eternal, as evidenced by last night's coup."

Jumaa paused, ensuring our attention.

"There are at least seven Islamic groups fighting for dominance. The most reasonable are promoting a coexistence with some level of democracy. At the extreme end, there are those who insist a representative government has no place in our country. They desire a return to the traditional ways."

Jumaa inhaled, as though steeling himself for his next words.

"Beyond the extreme there is the Shararaa."

"His last word," I said, staring at the corpse on the chair.

"That is correct. The Shararaa have been around as long as I can remember. They are limited in numbers but have become increasingly dangerous. They believe Sudan should develop no relationship with the infidel West. History has linked the worst of the political and religious violence that has occurred over the last twenty years to these terrorists."

"If you know all this, so must the government," said Greatrex. "Why don't they stop them?"

"The government's situation has always been precarious. They fear reprisals from the Islamic population if they crack down on the Shararaa, not to mention retaliation from the group itself."

"We've seen the violence that these people cause firsthand," I said.

"The members of the Shararaa are brothers. They are bonded through an ancient blood ritual. Their creed is vengeance without compromise. I suspect they've been planning to kidnap your vice president from the time his visit was announced."

Jumaa took a moment to glance across the room before waving a hand at the dead man.

"These people are not angry, impetuous rebels. The brothers of the Shararaa are highly intelligent, highly organized, and well connected in government circles. They will comprehend the ramifications of their actions."

"And they are?" I asked.

"They'll be certain that the West, your government in particular, will not negotiate. Their plan will be to gain strength and build momentum."

47

"What do you think they'll do, Jumaa?" asked Greatrex.

"It is my belief, and I am sorry to say this, but I'm positive that a publicized execution of Vice President Blake is inevitable. Most likely within forty-eight hours."

Jumaa's words hung heavy in the air.

I broke the silence. "Jumaa, you seem to know a lot about these people."

"Yes, I do," replied our friend. "I have had some experience with their leader, Atha Riek. In time, I will tell you more, but for now, let me say that these monsters are not alone in the depth of their convictions. At the right moment, it is my intention to explain to Riek, the profundity of my own beliefs, and to show him personally, what vengeance truly means."

Chapter 7

The morning sun blazed as we rattled through the streets of Khartoum in Jumaa's old Toyota.

"Are you sure this will work?" asked Greatrex.

"I don't see why not—it has worked for many before us," replied Jumaa.

More people roamed the sidewalks as the capital resumed its normal state of chaotic splendor. There was still some sense of unrest, judging by the concerned-looking faces deep in conversation, but tension appeared not to have escalated overnight. The three of us stayed at Jumaa's home and talked into the wee hours of the morning, throwing out one plan after another. Finally, the simplest approach seemed the best.

"The presidential-palace compound is only two minutes away. We must be ready. We won't have long before we're noticed," instructed Jumaa as he wrenched the vehicle abruptly to the left to dodge a local on a bicycle.

Greatrex and I took out our cell phones. We still believed that our most essential task was to contact the US government. That would now be harder for two reasons. First, we would not be broadcasting from the authoritative call sign of Air Force Two as originally planned—you can't just ring the president of the United States on your personal cell phone to tell him some unwelcome news. It doesn't work that way. The second problem remained that we couldn't call up anybody at all. The Sudanese authorities maintained the block on the internet and all cell phone transmissions.

Jumaa proposed a solution to that.

"Are you ready?" he asked.

Greatrex and I both nodded.

"Remember, political upheaval is so commonplace that our government has its routines perfected. While they have removed access to the internet for the rest of the country, they stay connected within the palace precinct. Every local knows that if you can sneak close enough to the palace walls, you should be able to piggyback the government's own services to get online. Their passwords are the worst kept secret in Khartoum."

Ridiculously simple.

One last corner and the majestic facade of the Sudanese presidential palace appeared before us. The building's huge ornate archways and bulbous domed roof imposed its presence on the city like an African White House.

"No signal," announced Greatrex, glancing at his cell.

"Likewise," I replied.

"I'll drive around the perimeter once," said Jumaa. "After that you must get out and walk. Too many laps in the car and the CCTV cameras will automatically alert the palace security force."

We circled the enormous building once but achieved no internet connection.

"Right," said Jumaa, pulling up at the curb, "out you go, quickly."

Greatrex and I bustled out of the Toyota. This seemed

like an absurd situation, but Jumaa hadn't let us down yet. We'd taken three steps along the pavement when Greatrex announced, "I've got signal." He then inputted the government internet password Jumaa had given us, the worst kept secret in Khartoum.

We ambled forward, trying to appear inconspicuous. When the big fella gave me the thumbs up and passed me his phone. I placed it to my ear.

"Hello," I said. "general?"

General Colin Devlin-Waters had been our commanding officer in Iraq. He also commanded our deepest respect. We'd rekindled our relationship when the now-retired officer had helped us out of an awkward situation in Iraq. If anyone could bridge the communication gap with Washington, it was our well-connected former leader.

As we walked around the boundaries of the presidential palace, I prayed that the internet connection would not drop out. I explained our circumstances to the general before pausing for his reaction.

"How the hell do you two keep wandering into these situations, Nicholas?" he asked. He didn't expect an answer. "We are aware there is a problem there in Sudan, but have received no details until now," he continued. "Are you able to stay nearby? I'll be back to you within the hour."

"We'll do our best, sir," I responded, "but it is a fluid situation."

"Do what you can, Nicholas, and stay safe," he added as he hung up.

Stay safe? I was considering how difficult that may be when I noticed two uniformed SAF soldiers strolling in our direction. I nudged Greatrex.

"I see them," he said.

We stopped walking, turned toward the palace building and pretended to look at the architecture. A couple of interested tourists. When we glanced to our left, we spotted another group of guards. They stood some distance down the road. One of them appeared deep in conversation on a radio. He looked up. A minute later, they began marching toward us.

"I suppose after we slipped out of the hotel, they distributed our description. I'd hoped they'd have more important things to do, you know, like dealing with the coup," I said.

Greatrex motioned across the road. Several buildings surrounded a substantial car park. There seemed to be enough laneways and other urban camouflage there to give us a chance to lose them. Before we stepped off the pavement, two more soldiers climbed out of a Jeep hidden behind the other parked cars. All escape routes cut off. Our fluid situation just became static.

"No flight option and pointless to fight," said Greatrex.

Across the street, the soldiers raised their hands to stop traffic as they crossed toward us. They gazed in our direction, narrowing their eyes like hunters preparing to pounce on their prey. On either side of our position, the SAF troops closed in, less than thirty yards away. I scanned for alternative escape routes. There were none. Vice President Jefferson Blake would be let down. Possibly the shortest rescue mission of all time.

Out of nowhere came a screech of rubber as a white Toyota Land Cruiser jerked to a halt in front of us. The passenger door swung open. I leaped forward and climbed in next to Jumaa. Greatrex jumped in the back. No one spoke. The tires screeched again, and we took off toward the heart of the city.

There was no gunfire as we sped out of the area. Any local soldier would have hesitated before shooting at two visiting Westerners. However, I was certain that we'd just upped the stakes for our pursuers. I prayed that the authorities had not yet associated the mess aboard Air Force Two at Khartoum International Airport with the two missing American musicians. If they had, the game would change... big-time.

"We need to disappear for an hour or so before calling back," I announced, knowing the impossibility of the task.

"I know somewhere we can go," declared Jumaa.

"Of course you do," said Greatrex from the rear seat.

"Getting online again may be the troublesome thing," Jumaa continued.

"I'm sorry to tell you, my friend, but we have no choice. That's a non-negotiable." Nicholas Sharp: immovable object.

Jumaa's brow furrowed as his face tightened. After leaving the immediate surroundings of the palace, he'd careered down a series of back streets and laneways, avoiding all police and military vehicles.

So far, so good.

"First, we need to get rid of this car. It will have become instantly infamous," he continued. "It's a shame—we've shared some marvelous adventures together."

Three blocks later, the back of the truck lunged sideways as we rounded a corner way too fast. Jumaa corrected and continued to speed down the narrow laneway. Although a dead end, he showed no sign of slowing down. I thought he'd lost his senses as we barreled toward a substantial stone garage at the end of the street.

"Jumaa!" I called out.

I should have known better. A second before we connected

with the building's two wooden doors, they opened, and we squealed to a halt within the dim space. The garage faded to black as the doors closed behind us.

Beside my window, a face appeared. To my surprise, it was a woman. I looked at Jumaa, who nodded. I rolled down my window.

"Nicholas, Jack, I would like you to meet my sister, Awadia."

Before I could say anything Jumaa rolled down his own window. Another face appeared; a child, a boy, perhaps about twelve years old.

"I am also pleased to introduce you to Awadia's son, Salim," he continued.

Subterfuge was clearly a family business.

Chapter 8

Jumaa's sister and nephew led us into the building through an internal door on the side of the garage. Their home was compact, but, like Jumaa's place, it appeared inviting. A homely, feminine touch was evident. Young Salim didn't take his eyes off us as he ushered Greatrex and I into the tiny living room. Pointing to two worn but comfortable-looking armchairs in the corner Salim said, "Welcome to our home, please sit down." Mature beyond his years.

Awadia and Jumaa sat on a couch opposite us. Our friend's sister had deep-brown eyes and a radiant smile.

"My brother has told me all about you," she began. "It is terrible, the developments at the hotel and then the airport."

I must have looked puzzled. Jumaa interjected, "I left my house early this morning to dispose of our terrorist's body. I also visited Awadia to inform her of our plans in case we required help."

I glanced at twelve-year-old Salim. He seemed unphased by the talk of dumping dead bodies. Perhaps *sadly* mature beyond his years.

"Would you like some coffee?" Awadia asked.

Jack Greatrex's eyes bulged with enthusiasm. Our hostess moved toward the adjacent kitchenette.

"Any ideas about how we can access the internet to receive instructions from the Colonel?" I asked.

"Nothing comes to mind," replied Jumaa. "It is obviously dangerous for you two to go anywhere near the presidential palace again. But there is nowhere else remotely close.'

"I will go," announced Awadia as she strolled back into the room with a tray of hot drinks. "No one will suspect a simple Sudanese woman of being a spy." She smiled a grin not unlike her brother's.

"No, not a chance," was our combined response, almost in unison.

"It is far too dangerous, my sister," said Jumaa. "I won't allow it."

I could feel the heat in Awadia's voice as she countered. "And who made you my keeper, brother?"

Definitive silence.

"You declared yourself that you have no better plan. I will go and that's the end of it." Awadia had concluded the discussion.

"What if your general won't speak to my sister, or he has too much specific information to relay?" asked Jumaa.

I gestured to Awadia with open palms. "When you contact him, mention the word *Kaitlin*. That is the name of his stepdaughter. He will know I sent you. Then ask him to send you a written message. I presume he'll have one prepared in case the signal drops out."

Awadia looked at me, confused.

"The general is a man who always thinks ahead of the game," I added.

I turned back to Jumaa. He didn't look happy but seemed to reluctantly accept his defeat. "Very well," he shrugged.

Ten minutes later, we wished Jumaa's sister luck as she left to catch a bus to the palace. In Khartoum a bus was the most inconspicuous means of transport. Awadia carried my cell phone in her bag. I had offered to instruct her how to use the messaging app, but she graciously declined me as unnecessary.

Salim looked apprehensive as his mother went, but he said nothing.

"All we can do is wait," I announced as we all returned to our seats in the lounge area. Waiting. I'd never liked it.

After spending two hours of imagining every potential scenario where things could go awry for Jumaa's sister, the sound of the front door opening snapped us out of our self-induced silence.

"Mama!" cried Salim as he rushed from the room.

A minute later, Awadia walked in. Salim was holding her hand. "It went well," she said. "Your General was receptive once I mentioned his stepdaughter's name. As you expected, he had formulated a message. I hope you don't mind, but I've read it." She passed me my phone.

The room returned to silence as I read the general's report. It was long and detailed. My shoulders grew heavy as I waded through the contents.

"This is big," I announced. "As the general mentioned in the first call, the State Department was aware something was amiss, but they hadn't appreciated to what extent. When they didn't hear from the vice president's party, they assumed it was because of the lockdown caused by the coup. He had protection. They worried but didn't panic."

"Perhaps they should have panicked, or at least reacted," offered Greatrex.

"The general says they sent two armed drones, MQ-9

Reapers from the US base in Agadez, Niger. This is when it got interesting. They were turned back by the air force."

"I cannot imagine the Sudanese Air Force turning away American planes," said Jumaa. "Not under any circumstances."

"It wasn't the Sudanese Air Force that turned our planes around," I continued. "It was the Chinese."

"Shit," said Greatrex, "that changes everything."

"Yes, the powerful show of Chinese took our people by surprise. The boffins at the State Department and the Pentagon were in the process of working out a suitable strategic approach when the general contacted them with our news," I added.

"So?" asked Greatrex.

"Then they panicked," I answered.

"Let's think this through," said Greatrex. "The US government now knows a terrorist group has kidnapped the vice president. They're also aware that several US personnel, including Secret Service staff, are dead. They should be champing at the bit to get in here and sort this. What the hell are they doing?"

"So, what does your general say that your authorities are doing?" asked Jumaa.

"Well, according to this message," I began, "they are pursuing every diplomatic means possible with the Chinese government. When they spoke to the Chinese ambassador, he denied any knowledge of their air force's actions. They also called in the Sudanese ambassador, but the problem there is that even he isn't sure if he has any authority to speak for his government."

"What's the president doing?" asked Greatrex.

"That's where things become concerning." I responded. "Again, according to the general, the US President is pursuing

58

diplomatic channels to settle this peacefully. He doesn't want to break through the Chinese Air Force blockade unless he has to. Starting a war with China would not be high on his to-do list. I reckon it would aggravate his heart condition."

"They've captured your vice president," said Jumaa. "Surely that counts as a national emergency?"

"There's the biggest issue," I said. "The president suspects the intel we provided may be inaccurate. He won't act definitively until it's verified."

"And it can't be verified until the US gets people and communications on the ground here in Sudan," added Greatrex.

"Which is impossible while the Chinese are blockading the county's borders," offered Jumaa.

"A particularly convenient catch-22," I said. "I don't know if I'm reading too much into this, but the bottom line here is that the president never really wanted Jefferson Blake as his vice president. He was forced into the choice by the scandal that involved Blake's predecessor."

"I think your president wants to be seen to be doing the right thing but is not overly worried which way these events turn out," observed Awadia. "He sounds like a callous man."

Jumaa's sister had summed it up in a nutshell.

"So, what does the general want us to do?" asked Greatrex.

"Well, there's the thing," I said. "Because no one else is actioning anything substantial, or is even believing what we arc saying, General Devlin-Waters has given us one specific task."

"Which is?" Greatrex was growing impatient.

I drew myself up in my seat before I spoke. "You and I are to locate the Islamic terrorist base and ensure the vice president's release by any means available."

"By any means available," repeated the big fella, "and with no support I suppose. Damn and shit."

"Indeed. Damn and shit."

Jumaa stared at Greatrex and then cast his gaze over to me. A small smile appeared on his lips.

"Musician's you say?"

Chapter 9

"We're not in the military anymore," I announced. "We don't have to follow orders. No one would blame us if we waited this out, or even headed for the border."

"As if," replied Greatrex. I nodded.

"Also, my new friends," began Jumaa, "I can offer you my assistance and that of my family."

"We appreciate that, Jumaa, but I suspect we are about to gate-crash a very dangerous party. It would not be prudent for you to become further involved."

I studied the man sitting across the room from me, his jaw tightening as his forehead creased. He glowed with grit and conviction. I suspected it would take some persuasion to convince him to sit this situation out. Before I could add anything more, Awadia spoke.

"It is too late for that. We are already involved," she said.

"There are risks," I replied. "We won't let you place your family in harm's way."

Awadia spoke again. Her voice expressed a quiet determination. "Salim, please go to your bedroom," she directed. "You have seen and heard too much in your brief life already, but the grown-ups must speak alone."

The boy's face displayed a silent disappointment, but as an

obedient son, he got up from the floor, hugged his mother and left the room.

"You have a remarkable boy," I said, looking at Awadia.

"Yes, I do, thank you," she responded, before reaching over to a side table beside the couch. She picked up a picture. When she turned it toward me, I saw a black-and-white photograph in a modest wooden frame. "And Salim had a remarkable father," she continued. "He doesn't have that father anymore. Our family has previously been in what you call 'harm's way'."

She passed the picture over to me. The man in the photo had a powerful face with eyes that blazed in defiance. I thought I saw a slight tear appear on Awadia's cheek. She seemed to will it away.

"My husband, Aathif."

Jumaa looked at his sister. Conviction had changed to concern.

"Normally I would not speak of this," he began, before gathering his thoughts. Our friend sat upright on the couch, thrusting his shoulders back. "Nicholas and Jack, you need to understand who you are dealing with, and you need to understand why we must be at your side."

Awadia glanced at her brother, offering him a silent nod of encouragement.

"The initial incident occurred twelve months ago, shortly before the fall of the government. My brother-in-law and I attended a place of worship. We took part in a scripture class to learn more about our God. As we left, we each carried a Bible. That was our crime."

Greatrex and I glanced at each other but did not interrupt.

"Two blocks away from the church, a police car cruised past. Aathif and I became the focus of their attention. They must have circled the block, because they reappeared behind us, at walking pace, following as we strolled down the street. We both figured what was about to happen, but by then it was too late to run. The officers climbed out of their car and began asking questions. Where were we going? Where had we been? Then they searched us, and found their incriminating evidence, our Bibles. The policemen shoved us into the back of their car and drove to the local police station. They interrogated us for four hours. They demanded to know the names of those in our Bible study group and if we had the support of any infidel foreigners. In our country, interrogation by representatives of the law such as those dogs included being punched, kicked, tied up, spat on and urinated on."

Jumaa paused again, gathering his strength.

"Worse than the physical pain was the complete humiliation," he added.

"You need not go on," said Awadia, no longer abandoning her tears.

"Yes, I do, my sister. We must talk about this, no matter how difficult it is."

"Anyway," he continued. "The police released us. We hadn't given them any names. We feared that if we had, they would arrest our friends."

"Or worse?" asked Greatrex.

"Yes," replied Jumaa. He sat there, staring blindly into the air, lips pursed. Finally, he added, "I'm afraid this story becomes worse. Much worse."

A cloak of silence enveloped the room as we all waited for our friend to continue.

"The second incident took place a week later. I should tell you that both Aathif and I attended university in Khartoum.

We'd been keen to learn about, and to be part of, the movement for effective change in our community. We were optimistic. As things turned out, we were also fools."

"In our optimism we had organized a Bible exhibition on campus. Our purpose was not to convert others to our faith, but to celebrate our beliefs with fellow Christians. You should realize that the Islamic government and security forces had people everywhere. They had young men and women attending the university. They appeared as if they were normal students, but it remained easy to identify them. In lectures, they wouldn't be taking notes—they would glance around the classroom watching the students, measuring our reactions to ideas and points of view. We considered them harmless. At one point, the fake students informed our group that the Bible fair would be viewed as a terrible idea. Feeling untouchable on the university campus, we ignored the warning."

Jumaa was in a daze, no longer present in the room. His memories had taken him to another place.

"At the end of the second day of the Bible fair, three of us waited at our bus stop outside the campus. Aathif, myself and our friend Mustafa. After the incident the previous week, we agreed to always travel in groups of at least three. We assumed it safer. It wasn't.

"Out of nowhere, a white pickup truck drew up in front of us. Several men jumped out. They wore no uniforms, but they had guns, and they made sure we saw them. They threw the three of us into the rear of the vehicle. Two of the armed men clambered in beside us. The pickup sped off into the night. Although frightened, the worst we expected was another beating. There is a saying in Khartoum, if a car is speeding, it is either stolen or it is government. We didn't believe we traveled in a stolen car."

"They cruised around for about two hours. Halfway through the journey, the men in the rear secured a tarpaulin over us, presumably so we couldn't determine our location. I thought that a positive sign. It meant we would come back."

I started to comment, but as a tear rolled slowly down Jumaa's face, it seemed better to let him continue uninterrupted.

"When we eventually stopped and climbed out of the vehicle, we'd parked in front of a massive, nondescript mud-and-brick building. There were no markings on the walls and no lights on the outside. I think my first realization that this might be worse than I thought occurred when the driver of the pickup got out. I remembered him as one of the policemen from the earlier incident. We'd been targeted."

"The officer stared at me, eyes wide and teeth bared, as though anticipating the misery he intended to inflict. I will never forget that. I will also never forget his self-satisfied grin as he said, 'I don't understand why you bother to go to university. You Christian fools are too stupid to learn lessons. Perhaps you should just clean my toilet.' Then he laughed, 'Christians used to be fed to the lions, tonight I will feed you to Atha Riek, the Leopard.'

"We were handed off to a different group of men who shepherded us into the building. No sooner had the front door closed than the lights flicked off and the guards hustled us down some steep stairs into a basement area. They locked us in three separate cells. There was no light, no toilet and no windows. It felt like the dark, dank depths of hell."

"I never saw Mustafa again."

We watched while Jumaa got off the couch. As he got up, his movement seemed awkward. I wondered why I hadn't noticed that before. He left the room, returning with a glass of water.

Awadia, who had been silent as Jumaa's story unfolded, said, "Brother, if this is too much for you, stop, rest."

Jumaa put up a hand to silence her.

"It was the evening of the second day when they came for me. I managed to keep a vague track of time based on when the guards changed shifts. My captors dragged me upstairs. Again, it was an area with no windows, only a bare light and some chairs. They ordered me to sit in the chair in the center of the room. Then the interview began. At first the questioning was slow, almost congenial, then the tempo built until it developed into a relentless barrage. 'Where did you get the Bibles? Who is sponsoring you? Is your local priest involved? Were there foreigners at the Bible fair? Are foreigners sponsoring you? There was simply nothing I could tell them. They lectured us about the US-sponsored Christian invasion, and how all good Sudanese people should remain truthful to Islam.

"When I couldn't answer the questions, the beatings started. It was the same as last time, pain and degradation. My increased resilience surprised me. I suppose this time I foresaw it. Only I didn't. The taller, stronger-looking man threw his arms up in despair and moved into the shadows at the back of the room. He returned with a whip. The handle was short, but the weapon had many strands. Before I could react, another guard grabbed me and lifted my shirt over my head. He hauled me forward on my chair. That's when the whipping began, over and over. The agony was beyond description."

"Jumaa," said Awadia.

"No, I will continue."

"Abruptly, out of nowhere, the violence ended, the four men

that surrounded me stepped back into the shadows. Then *he* appeared: Atha Riek. I recognized his face. Instantly I understood why he was known as *Al Fahad*, the Leopard. His eyes were a menacing deep yellow. His features were sinewy, but he looked strong and agile. Above all, I sensed his hatred."

"'Do you know who I am?' he demanded.

"'Yes,' I replied.

"'Then you will be aware of my reputation.'

"'Yes.'

"'They claim I'm ruthless. It's true, I have been brutal, but only to those who are the enemies of Islam. Tell me, Christian, are you an enemy of Islam?'"

Jumaa continued. "I didn't know what to say, so I just shook my head. I recall staring down, first at my trembling hands, then my legs, I had no control. I was awash with fear, not only for myself but also for Aathif and Mustafa.

"When I raised my head, Riek was smiling, as though he was savoring my condition. 'You now have two choices, Christian, what you decide will identify you as a friend… or enemy. You either give us the information we seek, or you lose your life. It's that simple.'

"There was no doubt to the man's sincerity. The trouble was that even if I wanted to, I had nothing to reveal. We had no Western sponsorship, our work involved no one from the US. We were just a group of friends and our local cleric. That information would certainly not satiate his rage.

"Suddenly, there was some scuffling outside the room, and then the door burst open. Two more of Riek's men came in. They dragged Aathif between them. My brother-in-law's face was a bruised and bloody mess. Someone had slashed his arms with a knife, and coppery red blood was oozing out of the wounds. He clearly couldn't walk, in fact, he barely raised an eye when I called his name. I can't describe to you, Nicholas and Jack, the abhorrent depths of my emotion. If there's a word that describes a cesspool of fear and fury at the deepest of levels, then it would describe what was boiling inside me.

"It was then that Atha Riek transfixed his gaze on me. I swear I saw the Devil dance in his eyes. Without warning, he drew a handgun out from his belt and pointed it at my forehead. I recall that despite his anger, Riek's hand was as steady as a rock. 'Speak now, Christian, death is waiting at your door.'"

Jumaa stared across the room, first at me, then at Greatrex. His sadness obvious as his voice quivered. "I had nothing, nothing at all to give them. I remember inhaling deeply as I prepared to face my God. Four or five seconds turned into an eternity. Then, out of nowhere, this madman swung the gun toward Aathif. Before I could scream out, he pulled the trigger."

"Each night, I relive the explosive crack of that weapon as it shatters my dreams. Each morning I awake to see Aathif's life disappear in a devastating mist of blood and bone."

The sound of Awadia sobbing filled the room with grief. I looked at the ground, not to hide, but to avoid intruding on this family's anguish.

Greatrex got up. "I'll make some tea," he said and walked out.

No one spoke for several minutes. There were no words that would help. Eventually Greatrex brought in the drinks and we sipped them in silence.

In time, Jumaa continued his story. "You are probably wondering how I am here to tell you this tale. Why did I not join Aathif in a savage death? I cannot explain to you the why, but I can explain how. As I sat in that room, shattered beyond any belief, they offered me a pathway. Riek told me that if I gathered information about the people, both foreign and local, who were supporting the 'Christian invasion', he would let me live. I had to become his informant. Of course, I agreed. Not to do so would have meant instant loss of life. I traded my soul to buy further time on this planet. I then needed to work out how to spend that time. The deal was that I would contact one of Riek's men at a football field in Wad Al-Bashir. I would meet them there three times. If by the third visit I had not given them the intelligence they required, my life would be forfeit."

Jumaa again looked at me. "You are speculating, Nicholas, as to what I gave them?"

I nodded.

"Well, at the first meeting with Atha Riek's men, they were late. I had to give the impression I was there for a purpose. To appear as though I was waiting to relay information was dangerous. I swung on the bars of the goal and jogged around until they came. If nothing else, it calmed my nerves. When they arrived, I was both relieved and scared. I informed them I was working on a source of intelligence and that I would have more for them next time. That bought me another reprieve.

"I couldn't see a way out of my predicament. My eventual death seemed a certainty. I went to my minister for counsel. He was a prudent man, and under considerable duress himself. He instructed me to tell Riek's men that he was preparing a detailed register of Christian sponsors for me to pass on. At the next meeting, that promise bought me additional time.

"When I returned to my minister after the second meeting, he said, 'Jumaa, there is no list and you have no choice. You must leave the county now. If you meet with Riek's people again and have nothing to offer, you'll be shot.' Of course, he was right. That night we started making urgent preparations for me to evacuate Sudan. By the grace of God, the social unrest that had been simmering broke over the next few days. Although the streets became violent, and we lost many lives, a miracle emerged among the bloodshed. There was a coup, and the extreme Islamic leadership was overthrown. Atha Riek would have suffered a loss of his support base. I decided to risk staying. I craved to carry on the work that Aathif and I had dreamed of, in his name... so here I am."

"You are a brave man, Jumaa," I said.

"I am a *lucky* man with a chance of redemption," he countered.

"You have nothing to redeem yourself for," added Greatrex.

"Maybe, maybe not," replied Jumaa. "I can, however, tell you one thing. If fate presents the opportunity to avenge my brother-in-law's murder, I will do just that. Possibly then, my conscience may be released."

The weight of Jumaa's words hung heavy in the ensuing silence.

A moment later he continued. "Since Aathif's death, I have learned more about Atha Riek than any man alive. So, I will teach you about him, I will show you how he works, and I will lead you to him. In doing this, I have only a single non-negotiable demand; when the time comes for Riek to die, I must be the one to kill him."

Jumaa looked at his sister. "That is why we are with you whether you want us or not."

Chapter 10

The dusky light was succumbing to darkness as we sped through the outskirts of Khartoum.

We were heading north east but Jumaa had not revealed our destination. We were perhaps placing too much trust in this man, yet every instinct in my body told me this was the right thing to do. After hours spent dissecting the general's update, Jumaa had suggested we drive through the night. A friend of Jumaa's had provided us with another vehicle; the aging Nissan four-wheel drive didn't look much, but it would do the job.

As we passed through the capital, the tension on the streets we had sensed earlier was building. There were many more people out. Most of them were roaming together in small groups or gathering in larger numbers on street corners. Several appeared engaged in animated conversation. It was also apparent that some men had armed themselves with homemade weapons such as pipes and lengths of wood.

"I don't like this," Jumaa observed. "There'll be blood on the pavement before dawn. I have told Awadia and Salim not to leave the house. But, on the practical side, it will distract the authorities, providing us with an opportunity to slip away."

So far that had been the case.

71

As we left the city lights behind, the road before us unfolded into a shadowed landscape of desert and mountains. We were clearly traveling to a remote section of the province.

"My contacts have informed me that Riek has been sighted in his preferred habitat. We are heading to the Batn-El-Hajar area," said our guide.

"Your contacts?" I asked. "Who are they, Jumaa? Where do they get their information? Can they be relied on?" The quality of the intelligence that we were acting on was paramount to any chance of success.

"Atha Riek is well connected," said Jumaa. "To survive, he's needed to have sources in the government and the military. Fortunately, through my own family connections, I also have sources. Sometimes his people talk, always my people listen."

"So, do you know exactly where he is?" asked Greatrex from the back seat.

"No, not exactly," said Jumaa. "I have an approximate location. When we get to Batn-El-Hajar, I'll make more inquiries, gather more information."

"What about the vice president?" I asked. "Is he with the Shararaa?"

"No one is certain, but my sources assume so. There is little talk regarding Vice President Blake."

"I don't know if that's a good or bad omen," I responded. "I just hope to God that Blake is still alive."

With that thought in our minds, we pushed on into the night.

Several hours later, as we feasted our eyes on a vibrant desert sunrise, Jumaa pulled the car over beside the bitumen road. The three of us had taken shifts driving, but it had made sense that Jumaa take over again now that we drew closer to our destination. The scene was spectacular. Long tracts of arid landscape gave way to a stunning mountain range in the distance. In the morning light, the mountains presented as distant blue guardians of the desert. It was big country.

"The Batn-El-Hajar Mountains," announced our guide. "They're quite something, aren't they?"

"They are magnificent," I observed. "I can't help but get the feeling that you're about to tell us that Atha Riek is somewhere up there."

"That is almost a certainty," said Jumaa. "The problem is Al Fahad and his men live as *noba*—nomads. They never stay in a single place for too long."

"So, our task is to discover where in those mountains the Shararaa have made their temporary base," added Greatrex.

"That's correct, Jack," replied Jumaa. "The trouble is, you could search those slopes for years and never encounter a trace of our prey."

I was glad that Jumaa was optimistic enough that we were the predators and not the prey.

"We'll head to Napata then leave the highway and push toward the mountains. There is a man I must speak to along that route. I am hoping he'll have information for us."

The Nissan's wheels spun in the dirt as Jumaa sped back on to the tarmac and headed north.

"Why does Riek use this territory as his base?" I inquired. "It's a long way from Khartoum."

"That in itself is one reason," replied our friend. "I think Al Fahad believes that the further he is from the central authorities, the safer he remains, but there is also another geographical purpose. We are drawing close to the Egyptian border. If events go wrong, he and his brothers can slip into

73

Egypt. The Shararaa will have allies there."

"So, is this Batn-El-Hajar a traditional Islamic stronghold?"

Jumaa laughed. "To be honest, the 'Valley of Stones' has been many things. Two thousand five hundred years ago, the Nubian kings and queens of Napata and Meroe built the pyramids in this region. Around 350 AD, when the Kingdom of Aksum invaded the area, the Meroitic Kingdom collapsed. Eventually three smaller Christian kingdoms replaced the Aksum. There are many Christian ruins in the territory. Move forward to the fourteenth century and Arab influence had grown throughout the valley. Islam became the predominant religion, as it remains today."

"Quite an evolving landscape," I observed.

"Yes, it is," replied Jumaa. "I sometimes wonder if that's another reason Riek spends so much time here. Maybe the fact that Islamic forces reclaimed the precious Valley of Stones from his Christian nemeses is a powerful motivation."

Ninety minutes later, we had left behind the sanctuary of the asphalt and were heading down a dirt road toward the distant mountains. The Nissan produced a plume of dust and gravel as we powered along. This was slower going, but Jumaa maintained a solid pace.

As the trail weaved through the desert, we started our ascent into the foothills. "In about thirty minutes, I'll turn off. I have a distant uncle, Ali Fake, who will help us. He is Muslim and well connected. He's an old man now, but was once very influential in the government, although no one knows why he quit state service. If there are rumors of the Shararaa in the territory, he'll know."

"Will he tell you?" I asked.

"Yes, we may differ in faith, but we have blood ties. We are family. Ali Fake is a trader. It's a role that gives him access to information. I hope he'll also be able to provide us with some additional weaponry."

We had escaped Khartoum with only the rifles and ammunition that Greatrex and I had taken from the terrorists the previous day. Our shortage of firepower was troubling.

"I'll certainly feel more confident when we're better armed," added Greatrex. "It's a shame we couldn't arm up before we left the city."

"I'm certain my uncle will provide for us," replied Jumaa. In reality, we had no other option.

It took us closer to an hour before we swung off the dirt road onto a rough sand trail. Jumaa put the car into four-wheel-drive mode and ventured on. He seemed to know where he was going. After another twenty minutes, a solitary structure appeared on the horizon.

"My uncle prefers to live and work in isolation," said Jumaa. We had pulled up next to a low clay-and-stone construction. The building's roof was flat and there were only two narrow windows exposed to the track. A four-foot-high mud wall surrounded the structure and the enormous yard on its southern side.

"My uncle may be a little hesitant in the presence of two Westerners. I'll go in on my own and talk with him, then call you to join me if all is well."

Jumaa climbed out of the car and strode up to the brick barrier. "Ali Fake, it is Jumaa Al Fadil" he yelled over the wall. "Come and speak with me." He was greeted with silence. I was becoming nervous. "Uncle?" he called again. "It is Jumaa."

Finally, the small wooden door in the center of the building opened. Jumaa walked through the gateway and up to the opening. We saw him shake hands with someone and then disappear inside.

Greatrex and I sat and waited.

"I reckon we've done some pretty stupid things in our time," he began. "But this just might be the dumbest of them all."

"If you mean attacking a terrorist camp on foreign soil with minimum intel, a couple of guns, and limited ammunition, I couldn't agree with you more," I replied. "It really comes down to choice, or lack there-of."

"Sometimes this Dudley Do-Right thing just gets annoying."

"And not for the first time," I replied. "To be constructive, Jefferson Blake seems to be a principled man, and he is our vice president."

A grunt from the rear seat. "We're putting a lot of faith in Jumaa," Greatrex continued. "We haven't known him long, and I don't enjoy being this dependent on someone we barely know."

"I agree," I said. "But what do your instincts tell you?"

"That Jumaa is a good man."

"Mine too, plus don't forget he saved our butts at the airport." Then I added, "Let's just hope that his resourcefulness will go the distance we need it to if we are to succeed here."

"Too damn right," agreed Greatrex. Discussion over.

Ten minutes later, Jumaa re-emerged from the house. He didn't wave us in. He stood in the doorway, his back turned in our direction. We could hear snippets of the conversation, presumably with his uncle, as it became more heated. By the end, both voices were raised. I looked at Greatrex in the rear seat. He appeared alarmed and was reaching down to pick up his gun.

"Just in case," he said. The door of the building slammed

shut and Jumaa returned to the car.

"That did not go as well as I had hoped," he announced.

"No kidding," said Greatrex.

"I'm sure it will be all right," Jumaa continued. My uncle informed me that word is, Atha Riek and his group are up in the mountains. He said they are being cautious and having minimal interaction with the locals. Even their supporters."

"Because they have Blake," I suggested.

"Yes, Nicholas, probably so. The problem is that whatever contact they have had with outsiders has been very threatening. Although my uncle has told me the most likely locations where we may find Riek, he wouldn't supply us with weapons. He believes doing that would guarantee certain death to himself and his family. Hence the argument. He also declared he would have no Americans in his home, *ever*. I fear, Nicholas and Jack, that the atmosphere here in the north is changing. Before it was uncomfortable, now it is dangerous."

With that, Jumaa started the engine, reversed the Nissan into his uncle's drive, and headed back the way we came.

The car's air-conditioning seemed to have no effect as the afternoon sun warmed the cabin well past the point of comfort. When we hit the original dirt road, Jumaa turned westward.

"How far?" I asked.

"We must travel for another three hours, at least. It will become slower going as we climb higher into the mountains. That, however, is not what is worrying me," Jumaa announced.

"I suspect what is concerning you, Jumaa, is what has been eating at me since we set off last night. If we do get 'lucky' and identify the general position of the Shararaa camp, how the hell do we approach it without being seen or captured?"

Jumaa nodded.

"And even if we manage that," added Greatrex, "how do we grab the vice president and make it out in one piece?"

"And therein lies the biggest issue," I said. "Everyone involved in this whole damn situation is acting in God's name. Atha Riek, his men, the Sudanese government, the West. Everybody seems to believe God is on their side. Go figure."

The shadows grew long as we wound our way up through the hills. Gradually the track became steeper, narrower and more uneven. The landscape, bathed in the deep-blue hues of the mountains and the vast views across each valley, was breathtaking.

I wondered if we would be alive to enjoy it on the way down.

Chapter 11

The intensity of the sweltering afternoon sun wore away at us, sapping our energy.

After four solid hours, it was surprising when Jumaa stopped the SUV on a narrow track just before a blind corner. Having not encountered another car or even passed through any village for at least two hours, we'd pushed into the most inaccessible regions of the Batn-El-Hajar Mountains.

"I fear my uncle's directions were not explicit enough to be of help."

"Do we have any chance of locating the Shararaa out here or has this been a complete waste of time?" asked Greatrex.

I observed our Sudanese friend. Over the preceding hour, he'd become quieter and his grip on the wheel tighter. His face now appeared drawn; his stress visible.

"I'm sorry, Nicholas and Jack," he said.

As he climbed out of the vehicle, our guide seemed nervous.

"Don't worry, Jumaa, we'll find a way," said Greatrex, sensing he'd been too abrupt. "This was always a big ask."

I studied Jumaa's face. An experienced sniper can generally read tells, the mannerisms that foreshadow a subject's movements. I had a bad feeling about this.

We clambered out of the car. The three of us stood on the

roadway as Jumaa opened the rear passenger door behind me. Without saying a word, he reached down and grabbed the Kalashnikov from the floor of the back seat. He leaned back against the door.

The stillness of the mountains was broken by the unmistakable growl of high revving engines.

"What the hell…" was all I got out before two open-top Jeeps, one ahead of us and another behind, came sliding into view, their motors roaring. Jumaa raised the gun, pointing in the direction of the Jeep in front of us.

"Fire, man," I yelled. "Fire!" Jumaa just stood there, rifle aimed at the man jumping out of the passenger side of one of the Jeeps.

Greatrex turned back to the Nissan to pick up the other gun, but Jumaa blocked his way.

"Step away from the car and onto the center of the path," came the instruction from the Jeep. Two sprays of automatic gunfire peppered the gravel at our feet. Greatrex and I backed up.

At least a dozen of them spilled out of the two vehicles. They were armed and disciplined, surrounding us in seconds. Each man held a weapon. Each dust-covered, sun-soaked face bore a look of weathered grit. Warriors. They wore no uniforms, but one soldier can recognize another despite their civilian attire. I looked to the man closest to me, his eyes a swamp of contempt.

This would not end well.

Jumaa stood there, frozen. His gun raised. He didn't fire, but neither did our assailants fire on him.

Greatrex and I remained in position with our arms raised. There was one remaining passenger in the Jeeps. He opened the door slowly and stepped out, towering above his comrades as he walked toward Jumaa. Those around him remained silent in deference. He raised his weapon, stopping inches from Jumaa's gun.

"Fire if you want, Christian, but you can see how this will end."

Any confusion about what just happened dissipated when Jumaa replied. "Tell Atha Riek that Jumaa Al Fadil is here. This is my third and final appointment. I have brought the Christian invaders that I promised."

The terrorist gazed at Jumaa without reacting. His distant stare lasted for several seconds before a broad grin exposed his uneven teeth. Instantly, the hot afternoon turned ice cold.

"Jumaa, I wasn't convinced you would come," countered the terrorist.

With that, he lowered his weapon as Jumaa dropped his.

"You received my message, then, Gataa?" said Jumaa.

"Of course," replied the other man. "We have been here waiting for the last two hours. Unlike me, *Al Fahad* kept faith that you would come." His eyes arced up and down as he assessed his prisoners. "He will not be disappointed."

Jumaa's face looked as relieved as Greatrex's did crestfallen. Everything flipped so quickly that neither he nor I had time to process the outrage, bewilderment, and disappointment that now coursed through our veins.

As the terrorists bundled us into one Jeep, a thousand thoughts rattled through my brain. How did we misjudge this man so completely? The signs had all been there. Jumaa's knowledge of Riek and his group showed way too much depth for him just to be an innocent victim. The rescue from the hotel ran too smoothly, tracking the rebel band too easy. How

81

did we not see that?

I considered the contradictions. We'd killed several members of the Shararaa cell aboard Air Force Two. Perhaps Jumaa didn't expect Jack Greatrex and I, two musicians, capable of such a lethal attack? That led to the death of the terrorist we interrogated at Jumaa's house. Perhaps Jumaa's whispering in his ear had been to tell the man that the rise of their cause necessitated his demise? Jumaa murdered him to gain our trust. Had he saved us from the Sudanese Armed Forces outside the palace for the same reason, or did he do it because he needed his hostages to come willingly?

The Jeep clattered slowly along the deteriorating track. We climbed higher, edging further into the mountains. Sitting across from me, Greatrex appeared despondent. We'd gotten ourselves out of some tight situations in the past, but this was different.

Despite the bleak outlook for our immediate survival, the betrayal dominated my concerns. Greatrex looked as though he felt the same. We'd trusted Jumaa Al Fadil. That had been a colossal mistake.

Again, I rummaged through the last twenty-four hours. The visit to Jumaa's uncle; that must have been to send a message to Riek, to forewarn him of our intentions and to arrange the ambush. The lack of additional arms available to us, clearly a set-up. Damn and hell!

If anything Jumaa said rang true, it may have been the story of his brother-in-law's death. I refused to accept that Awadia and Salim contributed to his deceit. But was I kidding myself?

All too easily we accepted the tale of Jumaa's liberation from *Shararaa*. It was now apparent that he'd still been in debt to Riek. Judging from the cordial response these terrorists showed Jumaa, he'd built up trust with the group as they waited for his bill to fall due.

There remained no doubt in my mind that Greatrex and I were to be the ultimate payment on that account.

The desert twilight cast long shadows as we heaved to a stop ninety minutes later. Our bodies were sore, and our minds fatigued beyond exhaustion. Perched high on a ridge, we looked ahead to a shallow basin surrounded by steep, arid hills. Through my dust plagued eyes, I perceived no sign of life at all.

"We are almost there, infidels," declared the terrorist seated in the front passenger seat. He then nodded to one of the two men squashed either side of Greatrex. The man raised his rifle. At first, I figured he would shoot one of us, but he pointed the gun to the sky and fired. Primitive but effective communication.

As we crawled down into the lowland of the valley, the road evaporated. No one would find you out here unless they knew precisely where to look. We'd never had a chance.

Eventually, as we rounded an extensive rocky outcrop, a sequence of tents, barbed-wire enclosures and vehicles revealed themselves. To the east, a precipitous embankment of granite rose above the makeshift community. Against its hard walls, several ladders led to what appeared to be caves.

It was Osama bin Laden and Al-Qaeda all over again. Bin Laden and his people spent many years hiding successfully from US forces in the mountains of Afghanistan and Pakistan. A complex array of changeable caverns allowed them to evade detection and extinction time and time again. Clearly terrorist groups learn from the successful modeling of others.

Everything in the encampment could be dismantled and disguised in a matter of minutes while key personnel retreated safely to the caves.

These guerrillas were experienced professionals.

Our convoy drew to a stop. Dehydrated and exhausted, I remained pissed at the whole situation. I carried little belief that our mission would result in success. Hope morphed into despair. Betrayal does that to you.

"Out," commanded the terrorist beside me, supporting his orders with a jab of his rifle. Resistance was pointless. The big fella and I clambered out of the Jeep. Sometimes, if you know someone well enough, you don't have to use words. Despite our enforced silence, a few exchanged glances said it all. We were both furious.

Behind us, Jumaa climbed out of the Nissan. He took a minute to look both Greatrex and I up and down. He then shook his head and spat on the sand at our feet.

"Take me to Al Fahad," he commanded the leader of the group. "I have nothing to say to these infidels." With that, the two men walked off toward the makeshift camp.

I sensed Jack Greatrex's venom as he glared at the receding figures. Greatrex is not a man who forgives easily… or forgets.

My own anger kicked at me like a raging bull. How did we let this happen? Drowning in frustration, they hustled us to one of the cave entrances.

"Up," shouted the leading guard before shoving me in the back, pushing me up a makeshift ladder.

"In."

Too many men with too many guns. We entered the cavern.

The space appeared small, only ten feet deep. Two of our captors, equipped with their favored Kalashnikovs, guarded the entrance. We may have been going nowhere, but at least we could talk.

"Don't even ask me what I think," said Greatrex. "I'm too pissed to contemplate anything but tearing that scrawny traitor in half with my own hands."

Jack Greatrex was not a man for whom the passage of time allowed for the dimming of emotions.

"That self-serving prick deserves a slow and painful death for this," he continued.

I knew from experience that the best thing to do was sit and wait while Jack let off steam.

Ten minutes later, after I'd said yes, mmm'd and agreed with the big fella several times, he seemed better positioned for a rational conversation.

"We need to get clear in our heads what's going on here," I began.

He nodded.

"From the comments we've heard among the terrorists, I reckon we can assume that Atha Riek is somewhere in this camp. It is therefore more than likely..."

"That Vice President Blake is here too," concluded Greatrex.

The big fella was back to his clear-headed normal self.

"Yes, he may be in any of these caves. So, even if we could escape our current situation, I don't know how we'd locate him," I said.

"We need to access some local knowledge."

"We do," I agreed. "The question is how?"

"And how the hell do we get out of this cave?"

"And if we get out of the cave, and get lucky enough to snatch Blake, how in God's name do we extricate ourselves clear of here?" Nicholas Sharp: pessimistic in defeat.

Silence.

Then more silence.

We eased our way back toward the cavern entrance. We'd previously moved as far away from our guards as possible so we wouldn't be overheard. Now I wanted to perform whatever reconnaissance was achievable from our captive position. There was no plan, not even a vague idea. Maybe checking out the lay of the land would inspire me.

"Not one more step," warned our guard as we approached the entrance. He emphasized the point by raising his rifle. We didn't need to be told twice.

Without venturing further, our prison cave still provided us with an unobstructed view across the encampment. It was an impressive vista. The valley appeared narrow but long. Foreboding rock faces surrounded it, although from our position, we couldn't see the other caves embedded in the same escarpment as ours. As the steep canyon walls curved to the east, I observed several other positions where there may be more holes in the rock. The terrain looked dry and uninviting yet held its own rugged beauty. Brave but unforgiving country.

At ground level, I noted six vehicles scattered across the area. That included our own Nissan. The terrorists' vehicles, all four-wheel drives, were sprayed in desert colors. Even with that, I sighted enormous sheets of army surplus camouflage netting nearby that would provide further cover for them in an instant. Two men stood beside the Nissan, already disguising it with the nets. As they threw the screens over, the SUV disappeared into the landscape.

Close to a dozen tents appeared randomly positioned throughout the immediate area, all covered in similar camou-flage netting. Most sat in the flat basin of sand adjoining the vehicles, but three were in a separate compound to the north, surrounded by a makeshift, yet robust-looking wire fence. The guards posted around the perimeter of the fence posed more questions than answers. What were they guarding? Were they stopping people from getting in or getting out?

As I watched, I started noticing movement on some outlying embankments and cliff tops. Despite the distance, I noted the glint of metallic weapons in the moonlight. A sniper's eye. The camp and the valley itself stood well protected. It would take an army to break in here.

We didn't have an army.

Each tent would serve a function. I assumed there would be a mess, sleeping quarters and conceivably even an armory. Greatrex made careful observations, presumably attempting to identify each. It had taken little to kick him back into military mode. It never took either of us long to make that switch. The fire that burns within never truly goes out.

After twenty minutes of surveillance, we returned to the rear of the cave.

"I figure the closest tent is the mess," said Greatrex. "I saw at least one fellow stroll out with a drink in his hand."

"The row beyond that would be sleeping quarters," I added. "I saw no one going in or out. Why would they if the tents provided only beds?"

"Agreed."

"Did you notice the canvas-and-rope structure out on its own and furthest from the sleeping quarters?" I asked.

"Yep."

"My guess is it's the armory," I said. "Far enough away to avoid accidents, close enough to be in reach."

"Wouldn't they be better off keeping guns and ammunition

in the caves? It would be more secure."

"I reckon that they'll have their substantive arsenal in a cave in another location. If this site became compromised, they would not want to lose all their weaponry," I countered.

"Then the tent would be their traveling stash, ready at hand."

"Exactly. I would sure as hell like to know what's in there," I replied, although I couldn't see any way we would find out.

"Now for the significant question," announced Greatrex.

"The compound. Three large tents inside and surrounded by wire and guards."

"What's that all about?"

"I've no idea. I didn't notice any people or even any movement, but there must be a reason it's there."

Nothing came to my mind or to Greatrex's.

"How many men all up?"

"I estimate at least forty, possibly ten more or ten less," I responded. "Either way, too many."

"Any ideas about how to get out of here?" asked Greatrex.

"Not yet, but I'm hopeful an opportunity will arise. If it does, we take it."

"Agreed."

"When I get my hands on Jumaa, he'll live to regret his cowardice."

"I appreciate that," I responded, "but for now I need to think… we need to think."

Our thoughtful silence engulfed the cave.

Chapter 12

It was dark outside when they came for us.

Erratic flashlight beams accompanied by hushed, urgent voices preceded our visitors. The leader of our kidnappers—the man Jumaa called Gataa, at the betrayal earlier that day—entered the cave. A guard flanked him on either side. One held a lantern, the other a Kalashnikov.

"On your feet. Al Fahad will see you now," he said.

To emphasize the point, the guard with the Kalashnikov kicked Greatrex hard in the thigh. I hoped he would live to regret that. I never liked bullies. We stood up, stepped forward, and descended the few steps to the ground.

"Walk."

We followed the guard with the lantern past the row of tents we had assumed were allocated for sleeping. Fifty yards ahead, we saw the glow of a campfire. A sizable group of men stood around it. I could hear shouting and laughter. Between the fire and the voices, these people showed confidence they would remain undetected in this location. Perhaps we'd find an opportunity in that. Arrogance could be a killer.

The guards stopped twenty feet from the cluster of men. We waited. A minute later, the men standing on our side of the group parted.

It took less than two seconds to identify Atha Riek. He sat on the other side of the fire, the reflection of the flames in his amber eyes making them glow. Cat's eyes. The man's weathered skin complemented the tightly drawn features of his face. He held his forearms in front of his chest. They appeared sinewy but strong. Even if I didn't know his moniker, the man's appearance would have suggested a wild cat about to pounce.

The surrounding men became silent, waiting for their leader to speak. I looked directly at him, captivated, searching for some form of expression, or perhaps a vulnerability. I'm usually good at reading people. With this man, I could read nothing, I could see nothing. The void sent a chill through me.

"Step forward, Christians." He spoke softly.

The guards at our rear manhandled Greatrex and I into the circle.

Riek's expression narrowed, his lips drawn tight like a wild animal anticipating a fresh kill.

"You have caused us trouble."

He stared down into the flames, his head tilted to one side.

"I do not know why you sought to interfere," he continued, his eyes still cast down, "but I'm certain you've achieved nothing."

The men around the fire remained silent, respectful of their leader.

Al Fahad looked up, his gaze penetrating. "You may be fools, you may be heroes. It's not important."

I'd never been good with the 'naughty boys being brought before the principal' scenario. I decided to speak. "Where is—"

My head lurched forward as waves of agony shot from the

90

back of my brain to the front. The butt of a rifle in the base of your skull will do that.

"Save what little breath you have. There will be no questions."

I struggled to remain standing, sensing Riek's eyes washing over me like a waterfall of jagged ice. I searched his gaze. It was as though no emotion connected him with the moment. A sociopath.

"Jumaa Al Fadil!" he commanded.

Jumaa stepped out of the gloom into the glow of the flames. "You have a final task. It will clarify your loyalty… or your fear." Jumaa nodded.

Looking up at his lieutenant, Riek continued. "Gataa, take Khalid and Mayen with you to the large cave. Supervise Jumaa Al Fadil as he interrogates these two. If he serves with honor, allow him to extinguish their lives in the most painful way possible. If he hesitates, kill them all, including Jumaa's wife and child." Wife and child? Jumaa had told us nothing about having a wife and child.

"Wait," I said. "What about Vice President Blake—"

The second round of pain hit the small of my back, then rippled up my spine. Nicholas Sharp: slow learner.

Riek looked at me with contempt. He nodded at the man to his right, who stood up and walked off into the darkness. No one spoke.

Several minutes later, two shadows appeared in the distance. The terrorist who had just left the group walked beside another figure. He was tall, with broad shoulders, although his gait belied his physique. He moved slowly with his frame arched forward. As his face emerged out of the darkness, I could see the bruising around his eyes. Trails of dried blood streaked down his cheeks and neck. A checkerboard of deep cuts encircled his arms, suggesting someone had been merciless with a blade. As he stepped fully into the light, it was obvious. Vice President Jefferson Blake had been having a very hard time.

"Sharp?" The strength in Blake's voice defied his current demeanor.

"Sir."

"How in God's name…?"

Riek turned to Blake's guard. An almost imperceptible nod between the two, and the guard raised his rifle above his head. Without hesitating, he brought it down, slamming it into the base of the vice president's neck. Blake faltered, but didn't go down.

The terrorist leader took a moment to survey Jefferson Blake's condition before rounding to focus on me. "You see where the power lies in our relationship. You would all do well to keep your silence."

Those around him nodded in agreement.

Al Fahad rose to his feet. He advanced a step toward Blake before sweeping his open palm in the vice president's direction. "How does the almighty United States of America look right now? What has your pursuit of arrogance and control bought you? Pathetic impotence. You stand here with the second most powerful man in your country bowed before me, his life in my hands. While my own government dances around with the conviction of a wildflower in the wind, I will bring America to its knees. Our allies, the Chinese will thank me, the Russians will be amazed, and my country will again live under Allah's protection."

Riek spat the words as much as spoke them. I'd been wrong.

This man remained totally connected with the moment.

"I am just one of many who stand for democracy—you can't kill us all," said Blake, his voice unwavering. The vice president was rewarded with a sharp punch to the kidneys by the guard next to him. Most men would have doubled over in pain. Blake stood his ground.

"While I may have some respect for your defiance, it serves no purpose," replied the rebel leader, looking again at Blake. "At the appropriate time, I will execute you myself. We've arranged for the event to be streamed to the world. There are others moving into place who are tasked to assassinate selected Western leaders. Your death is their cue. Together we'll sing a requiem for your way of life."

Atha Riek turned back to Greatrex and me. "I suspect that you two came to our country hoping that Sudan would join the capitalist economy in some type of market-based unification. Perhaps like your Ronald Reagan all those years ago… 'Mr. Gorbachev, tear down these walls.'" The terrorist leader allowed himself a slight grin. "Instead, I will give you a 9-11 moment. America's humiliation again, in the eyes of the world. I can assure you, the walls surrounding Sudan will remain standing for many decades to come."

Jefferson Blake gasped for air, but he had more to say. "You may kill me, but the US will react. Once our forces search you out, you'll be destroyed."

Al Fahad sat back down. His body crumpled into his robes, as though all energy had been spent. Once more he sought counsel from the flames. After some time, he spoke with quiet malice, his voice barely more than a whisper. "I believe you overestimate your own importance and the character of your president. He won't risk going to war with China to avenge a vice president he never wanted. He is not a man of principle nor conviction. I imagine a few heartfelt speeches, perhaps even a token coalition investigation. We'll be long gone."

"They'll find you," said Greatrex, speaking for the first time. "We are not a country that gives up easily." The guard behind him used the butt of his machine gun to strike the big fella hard in the back. There was a grunt, more of defiance than of pain.

Riek looked at him, his lips curled in faint amusement. "And how long did they take to find the great Osama bin Laden…? We'll disappear and reappear as we are needed. There are many powerful nations who wish to retain their influence in our region. Even bin Laden never had that level of protection."

I looked over at Jumaa Al Fadil. He said nothing throughout the entire exchange. Did Judas plan to take his thirty pieces and run? Maybe I was being unfair. The Sudanese man had betrayed us, but it appeared the lives of his wife and child hung in the balance. I wondered what I would have done in the same situation. Across the fire, Jumaa's features formed a mask of steel, his focus fixed on Al Fahad.

Riek inspected his group, as though assessing the commitment on each man's face. "Enough of this talk—we have work to do and an execution to prepare for."

Once more, I looked through the flames into the terrorist leader's cold eyes. Ice on fire.

Chapter 13

Once we were thrown back into our cave, we waited for at least another two hours, sitting in the shadows, talking through possibilities. The cold desert air seeped into our tired bones.

"If we walk into the place Atha Riek called the 'large cave', the most likely probability is we won't walk back out again," said Greatrex.

"I get it," I responded, "but at this point I've got nothing."

"We could try to take the guards out as we're moved up there. We'd only have a slight chance, but at the very least we'd go down fighting."

"You're right, the chance of success would be minimal. But that may be all we have."

Again, we sat alone with our thoughts.

Eventually...

"I can't get away from what is at stake here. The life of the vice president of the United States is in our hands, and our hands are tied, almost literally," I said. "I suppose the good news is that at least we know Blake is alive, for the moment."

"If we have nothing else by the time they come, we go for it then?" said Greatrex.

"Agreed."

"If it comes to that, I hope we can take Jumaa Al Fadil with us as we go down," stated the big fella.

I said nothing.

"Christians, to the front of the cave… now!" came the command.

"Here we go," said Greatrex.

We moved to our prison entrance.

"Put your hands in front of you."

As we did so, they wound heavy rope around them. Our hands *were* tied.

"Is this necessary?" I asked.

"Al Fahad does not trust you, nor anyone," replied our lead guard. "We're ordered to take no chances."

As I moved out onto the ledge to descend the steps, I saw what he meant. At the bottom stood eight guards, forming a semicircle. Each had a Kalashnikov. That made four guards per man. Once on the steps, I peered up at Greatrex and shook my head. There was no point. We were grossly outnumbered.

One hundred and fifty yards along the floor of the rock face, the guards stopped. A longer ladder leaning against the cliff, reached up to a ledge above us. It was lit from above.

"You climb," said the lead man. "One hesitation or incorrect move and you'll be shot."

I climbed up first. It was only twenty feet to the ledge, but with my hands bound and so many men pointing so many guns, it would be a terrible time to make an innocent slip. When I reached the top, Jumaa waited. With him stood the tall one they called Gataa, and the two other terrorists that Riek had demanded.

"Step aside so your friend has room," he instructed. His face expressionless.

Greatrex joined us on the ledge.

Gataa motioned his gun toward the cave entrance. "Move."

As we walked forward, this new space appeared to be much bigger than our previous prison. On the left-hand side burned a smoldering open fire, its smoke being drawn up through a natural flue in the rock ceiling. The implements sitting among the coals drew my attention. There were two pokers, three knives and a hook, all glowing red hot.

The guards followed us in. "Hold up your arms, both of you."

One of the guards unbound our ropes. That was surprising.

"Put your hands behind your back." Less surprisingly, our hands were re-bound.

Still standing, they tied Greatrex's wrists to a sturdy rail embedded in the earth in next to the cave wall opposite the fire. They pushed me closer to the furnace, its hot coals radiating waves of heat. One of the guards picked up a thick chain off the ground, its end attached to a link bolted into a large rock. He secured my hands to the other end.

"Jumaa," I said, "this is pointless. You know we have nothing to tell you."

"Silence!" screamed Gataa as he lashed out with the back of his hand, his powerful blow catching me full on side of my head. With my hands tied, I could neither defend myself nor block my fall to the ground.

Jumaa turned toward to the fire, reached down, and grabbed the wooden handle of one of the hot pokers. As he rose, he brought the implement forward, gripping it in front of his chest.

He read my apprehension as he stared down at me in the dirt. "I have no choice, Nicholas."

I stared at our former friend, his face contorted in concentration. Sweat soaked his forehead, pouring through his eyes and down his cheeks. He raised the poker, holding it above me. I had nowhere to go.

Jumaa swung the implement down toward my stomach. I prepared myself, muscles tensed in anticipation of the pain.

"You bastard," screamed Greatrex, struggling to break free.

All three guards watched on; no doubt ready to act if something went awry.

The poker was three inches from my gut, no need to remove my shirt, the hot metal would burn right through. I started to squeeze my eyes closed, but for a second I thought I saw…

Abruptly, an enormous explosion echoed through the cavern. Loud, but not deafening. A bright light sparked in the sky outside. We all looked toward the cave entrance.

"Go!" Jumaa instructed the guards. "Find out what is happening."

The three guards bolted for the opening.

Jumaa refocused, raising the poker once more. He glanced up at the guards on the ledge as he spoke to them. "I will continue here. Go."

He then turned back to me.

"Roll on to your front, Nicholas, now," he ordered.

I studied him, searching for some certainty.

"Now, I said." With that, he raised his left foot and kicked me in the side of my ribcage. It hurt, but also had the effect of rolling me over.

The guards started to make their way down the ladder.

"This is your last chance to tell me of your Christian colleagues here in Sudan," he yelled.

A second later, I felt the heat of the poker searing my skin. It stung like all hell. All my senses told me to scream, but the pain was fleeting. Then came the odor of burning flesh, only it wasn't flesh. It was fiber… the rope.

I knew it.

My refound confidence diminished when I heard Jumaa scream in agony. I rolled over onto my back, the ropes still binding my hands to the chain. The poker that had been in his hand had been flung through the air as Gataa had leaped over me and tackled Jumaa. The scream came because the implement had landed across Jumaa's chest. He jerked it off him as the guard pounded his face, punch after punch.

"I told Al Fahad you couldn't be trusted. You'll die here and now."

Jumaa tried to avoid the blows, wrestling his head from side to side. He was having no success.

Greatrex struggled frantically with his bindings. Another few seconds and Jumaa would have been able to burn through my ropes. We'd been so close.

"Die like the coward you are," shouted the terrorist, building himself into a rage.

Our Sudanese friend was having the life thrashed out of him.

I pulled and strained, trying to wrench my hands loose.

The guard continued his verbal tirade. "Your wife and child will soon follow you to your Christian hell."

At the mention of his family, Jumaa seemed to summon a last burst of strength, wrestling his right hand free. Instead of using it to hit his attacker, he flailed around in the dirt, searching… for the poker. A moment later, he found it. But without the benefit of sight, he grabbed the wrong end. For the second time in five minutes, he screamed in agony. The poker dropped to the ground as he withdrew his burned palm. He changed approach, kicking at the poker with his feet, unable to make contact. At first, I didn't understand his intent, but then...

I stretched over as far as I could, pulling against my ropes. Not close enough.

Jumaa had little fight left in him. He'd stopped trying to evade the heavy blows. Suddenly he gave one last kick. The poker shot forward, straight into my ribs. It felt like someone had shot me. Grimacing with pain, I rolled myself onto my side and edged back toward the tool. Two inches more. I smelled burning. The smell of rope fibers.

Ten seconds later, my hands broke free. I lunged toward the terrorist's back. He grunted but didn't stop his attack. I wrapped my arms around his neck and pulled backward with all my strength. It wasn't enough. I started punching, left, right, repeat. Each blow would have a devastating effect on most men. Although slowed, Gataa kept pummeling at Jumaa.

I released my hold and leaped backward. In two seconds I had the handle of the poker in my palm. Advancing forward, I once again wrapped my right arm around Gataa's neck as I plunged the hot poker into his side. I kept it there, pushing harder, deeper into him.

The terrorist's scream defined the soundtrack of human agony. The more he struggled, the harder I pushed. A minute later the strength seeped out of him as he collapsed into unconsciousness, splayed across Jumaa's almost lifeless body.

After untying Greatrex, we both bent over Jumaa. Breathing heavily, he lay there barely conscious and badly bruised. I found a pot of cold water at the rear of the cave, obviously used to douse the flames when required. I poured some into Jumaa's mouth and spilled the rest over his burns. He yelped in pain, but the water would cool the wounds.

Finally, his breathing became less labored. If I didn't know better, I'd have thought he was attempting to smile.

"Perhaps I should explain," he said.

Chapter 14

"I suspected from the start there it might turn out like this. I had hoped otherwise, but it is what it is," he began.

"Let's backtrack, Jumaa," I suggested. "How much of what you told us was true?"

"It was all true, Nicholas, every word. It's what I left out that turned me into a liar."

"You mean your wife and child?" asked Greatrex.

"That is correct, Jack. When they released me, Atha Riek said he'd give me three chances to make my freedom permanent, as I explained to you. What he didn't tell me was that by the time I got home, my wife, Salima, and my son, Ibrahim, would be missing. Al Fahad's men took them while I remained in their custody. They were his insurance."

"So, from that point on, the terrorist group virtually owned you," I said.

"Yes. I believed that they would never let me repay my debt. I'd heard reports about the Shararaa kidnapping the families of Sudanese men in order to get the men to act for them. The trouble being, I'd heard no stories about the families being safely returned. No one ever came back."

Jumaa stared at the ground, his lip trembling. "After what I've just done, that situation may well remain unchallenged. If there was any chance of their release before, it is now gone I have all but killed them myself."

Tears began to run down his cheek.

"I didn't tell you anything of my plans because I thought you would give yourselves away," he continued. "You didn't seem like actors to me."

"It begrudges me to say it, but you did the right thing, Jumaa. Atha Riek is a vicious bastard, but he is no fool. He'd see through any charade," I responded.

"Back to the story, Jumaa," added Greatrex. "When you realized Riek had your family, what did you do?"

"I'd do nothing to put innocent people in harm's way, so as I told you, I stalled and promised as much as I dared. I figured that something would come up."

"And it did, didn't it?" replied Greatrex. "We came up."

"That's right, Jack. As I mentioned, I'd spent a great deal of time learning everything I could about Riek and the Shararaa, including how they worked, where their allegiances lay, their contacts and supporters in the government. I was thorough. The lives of my family were at stake. I also built trust. It took time, but after a while, the Shararaa showed some confidence in me. It almost killed me to build relationships with the very people who held my loved ones captive."

"As Jack said, then we came along," I said.

"Yes. I knew nothing of their plans regarding the coup, the murder of the American agents or Vice President Blake's kidnapping. However, when I witnessed the two of you in action at the airport, I recognized an opportunity to strike back against the Shararaa."

"But you didn't tell us?" said Greatrex.

"Jack, I couldn't. It was too big a risk. On the way here my

103

uncle told me there was little chance we'd find Riek unless he wanted to be found. I knew with certainty I would need to change strategy. My uncle is well connected in this region, so I asked to send a message to Riek, to tell him the prize I carried."

"Us," I said.

"Yes, I'm afraid so. We would never have found the terrorist camp. I suppose I expected it all along really, so I made plans."

"The explosion?"

"Yes, Nicholas. I placed a timed charge under the Nissan. I suspected Al Fahad's people would search me, but I hoped they wouldn't search the car."

"What about the timing of the blast? You couldn't have anticipated that when we were at the bottom of the mountain."

"No," he replied. "That was why you had to be captured, but not me. Prior to coming up to this cave, the terrorists gave me enough freedom of movement to get to my vehicle and set the timer. They even made it easier for me to do this undetected when they covered the car with the camouflage netting."

"That's why you hesitated, right before you attacked me with the poker," I suggested.

"Yes, imperfect timing."

Greatrex and I considered what we had just learned. There was a ring of truth to it all. Jumaa's recent action had added massive credibility to his tale.

"I knew you hadn't turned," said the big fella.

I shook my head.

"All right, back to work," I announced. "We've found the terrorists' base and we've claimed a freedom—of sorts."

"Apart from being stuck in a cave with forty terrorists baying for our blood outside," added Greatrex, ever the optimist.

"Point taken. The blast will have sent them running all over the place, but only briefly. We've wasted too much time already. We need to get out of here, find the vice president and escape across the Egyptian border." Nicholas Sharp: strategist.

"One thing," said Jumaa. "I'll have only one chance to find my beloved Salima and our son. If they are in this camp, I will find them and set them free… or die with them in the attempt."

The magnitude of our friend's words was not lost on us.

"Of course," I responded, "but only if they are here, Jumaa—you must understand the chances of that are slim."

"Slim is the only chance I've lived with for many months."

Chapter 15

Our plan was simple and potentially effective. Jumaa stepped out onto the ledge in front of the cave to check what was going on outside. As he cast his eyes across the darkened landscape, his relaxed posture and lack of haste gave the appearance of someone seeking some fresh air. A minute later, he returned.

After informing us that the rope ladder remained well lit, and six armed guards still hovered around it, we realized there would be no chance of escaping that way undetected.

I scouted the rear of the cave in search of another exit. It took thirty minutes, but eventually I found a tiny crevice between two large rocks leading upward to a gap in the outer rock face. I tried it out. There wasn't much room, but the egress led to a ledge a good twenty yards away from the original entrance and the spotlight. This would be our way out.

We needed to sort out a plan. The plan became a short but perilous list: search for and extract Jefferson Blake, try to locate Jumaa's family, and get ourselves out of the area safely under the watch of at least forty armed terrorists. No big ask.

"If we can, I'd like to have a look at that compound we saw earlier," I said.

"Too many guards," replied Greatrex. "We'd be advertising our escape and we don't even know what's there."

I saw his point.

"I have a fair idea where Vice President Blake is being held," offered Jumaa. "I noticed a man taking a single tray of food to a cave opposite the compound. It appeared heavily guarded."

"How many guards?" asked Greatrex.

"At least four, one either side of the entrance and another two forming a perimeter twenty yards out."

These people knew their business.

"We need an order of events here," I said. "A timeline we can follow."

Both men nodded.

"Let's find Blake first. We're armed now thanks to him," I pointed at Gataa's body laying at our feet. "Once we have the VP, we'll do a slow search north to south for Jumaa's family."

"Our two biggest issues, apart from being outnumbered, are remaining undetected while we move around the camp and figuring out how to escape without forty killers at our heels," added Greatrex.

"Actually, I may have a plan for that," I announced.

Fifteen minutes later, we eased our way out of the small hole that exited the cave and dropped to the ground. While several of the terrorists combed the area where the Nissan had exploded, several others appeared to be traipsing through the darkness back to the mess and sleeping tents. At the base of the rock face, Greatrex headed west. I'd given him another job to do. Jumaa and I weaved our path north, using any available shadow or obstacle to shield ourselves from view.

A scant time later we lay flat on the ground thirty yards out from the cave where we suspected the vice president was being held. The guards were still there. That meant that Blake was probably still there too.

Armed, not only with the Kalashnikov we had taken from the Gataa but also two of the knives that were in the fire in the 'large cave', we crept forward. If circumstances forced us to fire a shot, an unwinnable firefight would ensue. Knives killed in silence.

"Jumaa," I whispered, "you wait here. I'll take the perimeter guard on this side first and then sweep around to the other one."

Jumaa just looked at me, eyebrows raised, as though he couldn't understand. "Not going to happen, Nicholas. I'll take the guard on this side, you swing around and take the other."

I stared at him. It was time to stop doubting this man's skill and resourcefulness. He intended to fight.

"Agreed," I said.

Crawling forward on my stomach, I made it to within five yards of the far perimeter guard. The rough ground required slow going, but it was the only way. The guard stood with his back to me, looking toward the cave. That was a mistake. He should have been scanning outward for intruders. I guessed, because of the late hour, he'd grown tired and inattentive. I crawled closer. My field training kicked in as though it was yesterday. Head down, gradual movement, don't brush any flora that would send a tell. I intended to try for another yard when the terrorist suddenly swung his head around. As he turned, suspicions raised, I leaped through the bush and shoved my shoulder into his chest, sending him careering backward. Before he fell, I flipped him around, covered his mouth with my left hand and plunged my knife deep into his heart.

He exited the world in silent submission.

I assumed Jumaa had performed a similar operation with the other perimeter guard. If he hadn't, I was about to step into a kill zone. Time remained an issue. At any moment, someone could investigate our cave and the ruse would be over.

Back on the ground, I slithered along the rock face until I lay ten yards from the cave entrance. I saw no way of taking the inner sentry without the other noticing. I slid further toward the closest man while searching for any clue that Jumaa was doing the same. Three minutes transpired with no sign of the Sudanese. I started doubting my decision to send Greatrex on a separate task. In fieldwork, Jack and I operated best together.

Then I saw it, a flash of white teeth in the shadows: Jumaa. We had planned for me to attack first, and Jumaa to follow. It didn't pan out that way. For some unknown reason, as I lunged at my man, the other guard swiveled back toward Jumaa. The sentry gaped at the figure silhouetted against the moonlight and raised his gun. Jumaa stepped forward saying, "It is only me, Jumaa Al Fadil, do not shoot."

The moment's distraction allowed me time to slip my arm around the terrorist in front of me and draw my knife across his throat. That same moment gave Jumaa an opportunity to close the gap between him and his victim. A moment wasn't long enough. He didn't make the distance. Jumaa's guard sensed something was wrong and tensed up, clearly preparing to squeeze his trigger. As he spoke in a calm, reassuring tone, Jumaa withdrew his knife from his shirt and in one fluid movement flung it into the terrorist's chest. A second later, he leaped on his victim like a wild cat on a kill. He wrenched the blade out of the man's ribcage before ending his life with a brutal thrust into his neck.

I would never underestimate Jumaa Al Fadil again.

The cave and the perimeter appeared silent apart from the distant noise deeper in the encampment. I put my finger to my lips. We needed a moment to listen harder. Two minutes later, it remained deathly quiet. I motioned that we should move forward… carefully.

Fortunately, we found no additional guards inside the cave. An oil lamp burning a low light lit the figure of Jefferson Blake curled up under a blanket next to the wall. I moved over to him, about to shake his shoulder when the man rolled over and landed a clubbed fist hard on my nose. I fell over backward, and he clambered on top of me. Just as he raised his arm for a second blow, he hesitated.

"Sharp?"

"Yes, sir."

"Shit, sorry about that."

On the other side of the cavern, Jumaa chuckled.

I gaped back at the vice president.

"I had decided not to give them any chance of a public execution and to make my stand here," he said.

"Not to worry," I responded, rubbing my nose. "We've got to move, sir—we have to get you out of here."

"No, I'm not going."

His words stunned me. Across the room, Jumaa looked just as shocked.

"Say again, sir?"

"I'm not coming, Sharp, at least not yet. Sit down for a minute and I'll tell you why."

I didn't have time for this, but I didn't have a choice either.

"Just to remind you, sir, there is a camp full of terrorists out there waiting to murder all of us with less than an hour until dawn and no guaranteed exit strategy."

"I know that, Sharp—Nicholas—and I appreciate the risks you must have taken to get to this point. But I need you to see the bigger picture."

The bigger picture. If there were two expressions I learned to hate through the years, they were *the bigger picture* and *the greater good*. I'd seen leaders use them too many times to justify no end of moral bankruptcy.

"Yes, sir, please explain... quickly."

Chapter 16

"I've had the advantage, if you could call it that, of being here twenty-four hours longer than you, Sharp. Despite these damn cowards' best intentions, I've had a chance to observe what's going on," said Blake.

He spoke with confidence and certainty, ignoring his injuries. I suspected he'd spent time in the same cavern with the fire and implements of torture that we'd escaped from. That can't have been good.

"Last night, I noticed a group of around twenty women and children being taken from one cave and walked into the compound at the northern end of the camp. At first, I thought they were the families of the terrorists. Then I realized that they were being moved under armed supervision. It made little sense."

I looked at Jumaa, sure that his mind was working overtime.

"Why did they shift them out of the cave at night and not during the day?" I asked.

"It seemed strange to me too," replied Blake. "Later in the evening, they changed guards. The new man that came on duty must have smoked too much bangu. The weed made him chatty. I had nothing to lose by asking him a few questions. He figured I was a dead man walking, anyway. Who would I tell?"

I nodded. Jumaa stood transfixed by the vice president's words.

"It appears the women and children are captives of the Shararaa. They won't let them out during the day on the off chance an aircraft or drone may fly overhead and spot them. Their only freedom is a little exercise at night."

"How long have the prisoners been here, Mr. Vice President?" inquired Jumaa.

"I got the impression they have been captive for some time."

"Did you get any intel on why they are here?" I asked.

"Yes, the guard had loose lips. He also seemed proud of their group's sadistic MO. It would appear that the Shararaa are holding these families while their husbands are blackmailed into committing crimes for their cause."

Blake observed our reactions, before continuing. "It gets worse. Not only is it morally incomprehensible that they hold these innocents as hostages, it also appears that the men of these families have undergone training in weapons and suicide bombs. It all made sense to me when Riek told us earlier that he has people moving into position to cause harm to leaders around the world. As he said, his trigger to them is the video of my murder. That is why I will not let him make that video. I will go down fighting first."

Jumaa interrupted, his voice low and quavering. "Nicholas, there is a possibility my family is with that group. They may be here."

I explained the issue to the vice president, including Jumaa's role in the entire affair.

"Good. Now that you three are here, there is a chance to help these people, however remote," said Blake.

I nodded. I knew where this was going and I didn't like it, but then again, I saw no other option.

The vice president sat upright and looked me square in the eye. "Nicholas, in all good conscience, I couldn't escape without attempting to save those families, not to mention the lives lost if Atha Riek's plan came to fruition."

Blake paused; just like the terrorist leader, he knew how to work a room.

"Could you leave them behind, Nicholas?"

I stared at the ground for an eternity. Finally, I raised my head, fixing my gaze on Jumaa. My Sudanese friend's eyes were wide open, his lower lip trembling.

"No, sir, I could not."

And with that response, I believed I'd just delivered a death sentence to us all.

We crept across the landscape in front of Blake's former prison. Although there was nothing to indicate the terrorists had heard our escape, it would only be a matter of time. Someone would investigate the silence from the torture cave soon, and then the shit would hit the fan.

Our immediate aim was to make it to the compound undetected, immobilize the guards, and break in. Simple. At least three was better than one. Even in his battered state, Vice President Jefferson Blake hadn't forgotten his military training. He was now part of the team.

From a mound twenty feet from the south-west corner of the enclosure, we managed to gain a decent view of the security arrangements. In the moonlight, we saw no movement within the wired area. Then I considered the tents.

"They may have moved them out here to avoid hearing our

supposed torture," I suggested. "They must be in those tents. The guards wouldn't protect an empty compound."

"Makes sense," said Jumaa.

Blake nodded.

I'd given Jefferson Blake my gun and kept the knife. I daren't leave the vice president of the United States unarmed. That one of the prime goals of my mission here was to bring Blake back alive weighed in my thoughts, but I didn't think it weighed that heavily in his own thinking. That spoke to the measure of the man.

Four guards covered the entrance to the compound and two more on each corner. They looked out, not in.

"I'll work my way around to the north east," I said, "then I'll try to take those two out and cut my way in. You both stay here."

"No," said Blake. "You'll have twice the chance with the two of us. I'm coming with you."

His offer didn't surprise me.

"All right, accepted. Jumaa, you keep an eye on the guards on the gate. If we get in, we'll try to make it to the tents. If we can, we'll bring any hostages out the way we went in," I instructed.

I worried that at any moment Riek's men would uncover our absence. Every minute counted. The terrorists hadn't taken my watch, nor Greatrex's. They probably figured they would remove them from our corpses later on. Less fuss. I glanced at mine. Whether or not our escape remained undiscovered, I knew that Jack Greatrex would action his part of the operation in less than ten minutes if he'd been able to make his position. If he failed, we would walk to a certain death.

Jefferson Blake and I made our way round to our proposed

point of entry. I indicated the guard closest to him as the man to take, before swapping my knife for his gun. He'd have a greater chance with the knife. After we both got in position five yards away from the guards, I counted down on my hand. On cue, we both advanced.

I hit trouble within a second. My guard must have heard something crack under my foot. He swiveled round and raised his weapon. I dove to the left. We couldn't afford the sound of gunfire. Besides, I didn't want to be shot. Nicholas Sharp: moving target.

I rolled on my shoulder and sprung back up at him. My opponent reacted quickly, his rifle zeroing in on me while he was still out of arm's reach. I had nowhere to go. I surged ahead in one last futile attempt to disarm him, knowing the pain coming my way.

Unexpectedly, the terrorist lurched forward toward me. I wondered why he hadn't fired. Then I saw the blade sticking out of the side of his ribs and Jumaa half-hidden behind a bush.

"Sorry, Nicholas. I'm aware you were a military man, but orders aren't really my thing. If my family is in there, he pointed at the compound, I want to get them out."

I should have known.

Jefferson Blake encountered no issues with his target. As I looked over, the guard lay prone on the ground. From the amount of blood seeping into the surrounding sand, he wasn't going anywhere.

"Let's move," I said.

We slipped under the wire using the tents in the middle of the compound as cover as we sprinted toward the remaining guards.

Now we all held guns. Blake passed me the blood-soaked

knife, and I sliced an entrance into the first tent. I pushed through the gap with Jumaa breathing down my neck. It was empty.

It was the same result with the second tent. I glanced at Jumaa. The man's closed eyes and sagging shoulders spoke of his fading hope. As we came to the third tent, there was a sound, perhaps a whisper. Jumaa got there before me and cut a long strip through the canvas. He dove into the darkness.

Blake and I were seconds behind him going in. As we entered the space, we saw around twenty pairs of eyes glowing at us. They were all wide with fear.

Jumaa spoke with a soft desperation. "Salima, Ibrahim, *ita hena*? Are you here?"

A muted cry came from the rear of the tent. A tall woman ran forward, her movements sharp and forceful as she broke through the crowd. The muted cry became a howl of pain, her face crunched in uncontrolled emotion. As I prepared to block her way, she threw her hands in the air, her voice trembling as she cried, "My husband, my husband."

Jumaa exploded into her arms. "Ibrahim, is he here?"

"Safe and well, but scared," she responded. Another woman passed a small child forward.

Jumaa crumbled, dragging his wife to her knees. Tears streaked down his cheeks. Both Blake and I stepped back to give the family a brief moment. It turned out brief was all they had.

Yells erupted from the camp, followed by a burst of automatic gunfire. The terrorists had discovered our escape. If we'd only had another five minutes...

Chapter 17

"Jumaa, lead these people out the way we came in, stay down!"
I ordered, keeping my voice low but urgent.

He'd already begun moving.

I turned to Blake. "Sorry to give orders above my paygrade,
sir, but it's how it's got to be."

"Understood."

"If you cover the rear of Jumaa's group, I'll try to distract the
guards at the gate. With a little luck, they won't have realized
we're in the compound. In their eyes, we have no reason to be
here."

Blake looked at me for a second. "Be careful, Sharp." Then
he disappeared into the night.

I stepped out, working my way around the side of the tent.
All the compound sentries headed toward the main camp or
gawked in that direction. Jumaa's people had almost made it
across the exposed area when one terrorist glanced over his
shoulder and spotted them. The man stood too far away for
me to use a knife. I raised my gun, aimed and shot. He let out
a warning scream as he crumpled to the ground, but by then
it didn't matter.

I adjusted the selector switch from semi-automatic to
automatic and fired off two bursts. Three guards down, but

my firing had alerted the guards by the primary compound gate to my presence. They opened fire. I hit the sand and rolled back behind the tent. Its fabric walls instantly became a mess of shredded canvas, offering little or no cover.

Peering over my shoulder, I realized my gunfire had allowed the others to escape. Now I just had to keep the terrorist's attention on me. Staying low, I crawled over to the second tent but didn't stay there long. As the next rounds tore through the canvas, I got up and sprinted toward the third tent, spraying the guard's position with fire. Bullets kicked up the surrounding sand, but I made it. I figured the guards would think I'd advance along the northern side.

I counted to ten. A burst of gunfire splattered the ground in the direction that they thought I would attack from, but I wasn't there. I doubled back to what remained of the second tent, ran to the far wall and came straight at them. The two seconds it took for the terrorists to realize they had made a mistake was all I needed. They paid with their lives.

I inhaled three lengthy breaths before sprinting after Jumaa, Blake, and the women and children. They'd reached the sparse scrub by the time I caught up with them.

"What do you have in mind, Sharp?" asked Jefferson Blake.

"If we just keep heading into the desert, the terrorists will regroup and round us up at daybreak," I said. "Everything depends on Jack Greatrex."

The words had barely left my mouth when the first explosion lit up the sky. Then a second. Two of the tents that the Shararaa used as sleeping quarters disappeared in flames. The odds were evening up.

"Run!" I shouted at the group, pointing to the cars. "Jumaa, the vehicles, go!" Our Sudanese friend didn't need to be told twice.

The encampment was now awash with frenzied activity. People were screaming orders and others were firing blindly into the night.

We bolted toward the area where we had first arrived earlier in the day, staying free of the reflected firelight.

At the halfway point I yelled at Blake, "I'm detouring to find Greatrex, I'll meet you at the cars."

The vice president just raised an arm as he fled. He knew that protecting the families remained his priority.

As I rounded the mess, I expected the canvas armory to be lit in a sea of flame. That had been the plan. Instead, the tent stood intact. I was confused, but that wasn't the only surprise the big fella had in store. With one flap lifted, I made out two metal barrels pointing out of the darkness. I veered to the right to avoid being caught in the firing line. A second later, one of the four-wheel drives in the center of the camp, well away from where the women and children were headed, exploded into flames.

The second weapon fired. Two hundred yards away, a group of terrorists huddled in attack formation evaporated. How in God's name… I didn't comprehend what Greatrex had in there, but he sure as hell wreaked a truckload of havoc.

As I surveyed the scene before me, it was clear Greatrex couldn't last forever in his current situation. His rearward sector remained exposed. It wouldn't take the terrorists long to regroup enough to outflank him and attack from behind.

While every fiber of my being urged me to leap forward and engage in the fight, experience told me that would be a mistake. A sniper's job is to remain detached and focused. Protect the men in the field; that's core business. I felt a familiar calm as I crouched down and raised my weapon. From my position, I'd cover Greatrex while he kept firing. At least for a few minutes. He'd do a lot of damage in that time.

I spotted the first terrorist a minute later. He came in low, crouching but not crawling. That was a mistake. I flicked the selector switch on the Kalashnikov back to semi-automatic and took aim. No chance for preparation. A quick intake of breath and a gradual exhale. Squeeze the trigger. One less bad guy.

Greatrex would have heard the gunfire. I hoped he realized my strategy.

Two more shadows moved in the dark. They were coming in directly behind the big fella's location. Smarter than their predecessor, they slithered on their bellies, almost undetectable. Before they could get any closer, Greatrex fired another shot; a second vehicle exploded up in flames. The action seemed to enrage his stalkers. They rose and charged forwards. Another mistake. Two rapid shots and I killed them both.

A bunch of people were dying before my eyes, but they weren't good people. I thought briefly about the damage this group of religious extremists had inflicted on so many families. The bloody road I traveled didn't lead to guilt.

I figured by this point that about half the terrorists had been taken out. That still left twenty, minimum, without counting outliers who guarded the valley. The odds remained stacked against us.

Greatrex fired two more rounds. He'd have more than one grenade launcher in there, but they took time to load. That made him vulnerable. I saw more figures approaching, not only from the rear but also from the southern side. I didn't have a clear shot at every one.

I jumped to my feet and shouted, "Jack, on your three." If he heard me, he'd know what to do. I then flicked the selector back to automatic and sprayed the scrub behind the ammunition tent. Dropping to the ground the moment I stopped firing, I set about picking off any survivors one by one.

The big fella must have taken note because a barrel swiveled round ninety degrees. He shot straight through the canvas wall of the armory, wiping out his attackers.

I ran toward his position. He stepped from the tent sweaty, out of breath and wearing a decidedly self-satisfied grin. "We've pushed our luck," I yelled. "Let's go."

Greatrex raised an eyebrow when he saw me, but he didn't need any further persuasion. He reached behind, picked up a small canvas bag and sprinted in my direction. I pointed ahead to where Jumaa and Blake had taken the women and children.

As I caught up with him, I shouted, "What the hell did you have in there?"

He smiled like a Cheshire cat. "A couple of Chinese QLZ-87 35mm ATLs. Freakin' effective."

Jack loved his guns. As we bolted across the sandy terrain, I craned my head back to the ammo dump, observing Riek's men swarming around it.

"I don't suppose…"

"Sure did," replied the big fella.

Ten seconds later, we felt the explosion shake the ground as the flames from the terrorists' armory rose thirty feet into the darkness.

Chapter 18

We weren't out of the woods yet, but now we had an opportunity. By the time we reached the vehicles, Jumaa had the camouflage netting off two of the vehicles.

"Jumaa, get everyone into the Land Rover and the long-based Jeep next to it. It'll be tight."

I ran around to the front of both cars. The Land Rover had its keys still in the ignition, and it took me all of five seconds to hot-wire the Jeep.

"Where's Blake?" I asked.

"Once we got here safely, he went back to help. I assumed he was with you."

"Shit," it appeared the vice president wasn't much good at following orders either.

"Into the car now, everyone," I yelled.

"What about Blake?" asked Greatrex.

"You guys get going, take these people out of here. I'll go back for him."

"I'm coming."

"No, you need to drive, now move the hell out of here."

Damn it all.

Suddenly, a rattling spray of bullets pounded the Jeep's tailgate. I whirled, firing a burst blindly into the darkness.

I tried to fire again, but all I heard was the click of an empty chamber.

Like ghosts in the blackness, four figures appeared out of the shadows. They all had automatic rifles pointing at the women and children.

"Put your weapons down now."

It was Atha Riek.

We'd come so close.

There wasn't much to say. No negotiation would get us out of this, we had no choice but to drop our weapons. I glanced behind me. The youngsters were crying, their mothers staring helplessly at the terrorist who had been their captor for so long.

If I was going to die at this moment, it wasn't going to be without a fight, but I just couldn't figure out where to begin.

The man on Riek's left carried a heavy wound in his shoulder. I hoped I'd done that. The two terrorists on his right looked unscathed. From his furrowed brow and twisted grin, it was clear Riek was pissed.

"Nicholas, please comfort that young girl to your left." Jumaa's voice sounded more agitated than conciliatory.

About a foot behind me a small girl, around six years old, was sobbing. I appreciated Jumaa's intent, but I didn't want to make the child into a target any more than she already was. Then I figured it out. Nicholas Sharp: slow on the uptake.

I edged to my left. Before I had taken a second step, Jumaa pulled the knife from his belt and hurled it. The blade hit Atha Riek in the stomach, blood pouring from the wound as he lurched backward. The terrorist's surprised offsiders gaped before reacting.

The big fella had also foreseen Jumaa's intentions; before

the two terrorists on Riek's right got off a shot, Greatrex dived to the ground, swept up his gun and cut them both down in a burst of automatic fire. I heard the familiar hollow click as he ran out of ammunition. It didn't matter. I lunged forward and grabbed Riek's remaining man in a headlock, punching into his wounded shoulder repetitively. Within a few seconds, the pain rendered him unconscious.

Before I was able to pick up the terrorist's weapon, more gunfire echoed close by. Atha Riek was standing, clutching his stomach with one hand, his Kalashnikov with the other. He was staring fixedly at Jumaa who was lying against the Land Rover's front wheel, his upper leg now a bloody mess.

Riek risked a glance at me. "You reach for that gun Sharp and ten children plus that traitor will be dead by the time you touch it." He spat the words as he eyed up Jumaa's helpless frame.

Greatrex grunted in disgust but could do nothing either except shield the kids. His wide eyes glowed with hatred.

There was nothing I could do at all.

Riek took a deep breath, wincing in pain. "Jumaa Al Fadil, you'll be the first to die. No God, yours or mine, will provide sanctuary for a traitor like you." He spat out the words through gritted teeth as he aimed his gun at Jumaa.

"Do not talk to me of betrayal, you filthy animal." Jumaa spoke with force and conviction, although clearly struggling for breath. "You speak of God as though his cause is your cause. You have no cause." Our Sudanese friend paused. From his drawn skin and semi-closed eyes, it was clear every word he spoke came at a cost. "Across our land, men and women have united for peace. Muslims and Christians alike, all good people, all speaking with a solidarity that you will never understand. You have betrayed them all. Every day I am haunted by the death of my brother Aathif. You betrayed his wife, his son, our entire family when you took his life for the sake of your own power. Don't you dare call me a traitor. *Amashi al-nar*—go to hell!"

"Quiet," responded the terrorist leader.

Jumaa took a deep breath, his features relaxing. He looked relieved to have spoken his peace as he prepared himself for a certain death.

Al Fahad smiled, his cold eyes showing the empathy of stone. "Be gone," he growled as his finger tightened on the trigger.

The shot rang through the silence, everyone gasped.

The terrorist's stony look was cast in frozen permanence as his eyes rolled back in their sockets. A geyser of blood erupted from the side of his head as he fell to the ground.

"I never did like bullies," said Jefferson Blake as he lowered his gun.

Chapter 19

The two packed vehicles descended the treacherous mountain trail with care. Greatrex had either blown up or disabled the terrorists' remaining transport. In the back of my mind I was acutely aware of the Shararaa stationed around the rim of the valley, and wondered what means of transportation they had access to – they would have heard the blasts, even if they didn't know what was going on yet.

I drove the roofless Jeep while Blake rode shotgun. Greatrex drove the Land Rover behind us. Our greatest worry was Jumaa, who was laying down in the back of the Jeep. His leg had been bandaged as best we could, but he was losing a lot of blood. We'd need to find him medical attention soon. His wife, Salima, was nursing him, while his son, Ibrahim, looked on. Their pursed lips and wrinkled brows were a picture of concern.

Our nerves drawn tight, we approached the entrance to the valley. This was the spot where the terrorists had signaled our arrival and communicated through gunfire. They would be on alert, but would they act without their leader? Driving with our lights off made our progress difficult, but there was no point in advertising our presence.

Blake had his eyes peeled to the ridges, looking for any sign of movement. So far, he saw nothing.

"Maybe the lookouts returned to the camp when they heard the shooting and explosions?" suggested the vice president.

"It's possible," I said, "but we haven't encountered any on the track. I don't reckon there are too many alternative roads around here. If we make it clear of the valley, we'll need to turn on the lights and go for it. Jumaa will not last the distance at this rate."

Just as I was starting to feel some level of confidence, we rounded a sharp corner to find a pickup parked across the track. No one was in the vehicle or in sight. This was a trap.

"Eyes up," I shouted.

There was little time to make a decision. The terrorists would expect us to stop. It would be the natural thing to do.

"Hold on," I yelled as I floored the gas pedal.

We rammed the back fender of the pickup ahead. It was the lightest section of the vehicle and easiest to move. The grille guard on the front of our car impacted loudly on the pickup. After the initial thump, the other vehicle slid awkwardly across the track toward the cliff.

We were halfway through the maneuver when the first gunshot rang out. It was Greatrex. I flicked on the lights just as an enormous man with a Kalashnikov stepped out from the shadow of rock just in front of us. I raised my now reloaded gun over the windscreen and fired. He fell forward onto our hood before bouncing off and sliding under our wheels, his groan audible.

More firing sounded behind us before Jefferson Blake sprung to his feet, aimed his gun and pulled the trigger. To my right, I saw one of our would-be attackers, who had been hiding on the other side of the stationary pickup, stumble backwards and cascade over the lip of the cliff.

Metal screeched as we scraped the side of the terrorist vehicle, now tottering on the precipice. I braked hard, then floored the gas pedal once more. The contact sent the terrorist's pickup toppling down into the valley. The explosion was audible as it hit the rocks below.

I gunned it out of there.

Ten minutes later, I pulled over to check on our passengers.

"I think there were only three of them, including one I tapped on the hill," said Greatrex. "We didn't take a hit."

"I hope that's the last of them," I responded. "Lights on and traveling as fast as we can from here on in, for Jumaa's sake."

Greatrex nodded. We clambered back to our vehicles and pushed on.

As the desert sun rose over the peaks, the flaring orange beams of sunlight struck like lightsabers over the blue hue of the mountains. This was magnificent country. If we hadn't been fleeing from a night of bloodshed with terrorists barking at our heels, it could have been a stunning moment.

But the only beauty I was appreciating as we thundered down the tracks was the fact we had survived the night and been able to rescue our innocents.

"We need to decide soon, Mr. Vice President. Do we try to cross the border with the women and children or find them a secure refuge in-country before we leave?"

"I've been contemplating that very thing, Nicholas. I'm not convinced there's a decision to make," Blake responded.

I knew where this was going.

"There is nowhere safe in Sudan for these people," he continued. "Atha Riek may be dead, but his group had a very broad reach. We've cut off the head of the serpent, but a fresh one will emerge. If for no other reason than revenge, they will come after these families. We have to get them out."

"To the US?" I asked.

"Yes, somewhere we're able to protect them. I've got contacts in the government, you know."

Blake grinned. I laughed. It had been a while.

"Okay," I responded. "First step, we need to get Jumaa some decent medical treatment. He won't survive the journey without hospital care. If he lays up for a few days, we can send someone back in to pick him up."

"I understand there is a hospital in Wadi Halfa. That's on the Nile, close to the Egyptian border. We could bug out from there, although I'm unsure how far it is."

"Sounds like a plan. I reckon we drive for another couple of hours, get our bearings, and health check Jumaa," I replied.

"Now I don't want to rain on our parade, but have you got any ideas regarding a way to contact our government en route?" asked the vice president.

"Yes, sir, Jack Greatrex has an idea about that."

Jefferson Blake turned to look at me. "You two are very resourceful. What you've done tonight has been impressive."

"Thank you, sir, but don't under value your own contribution."

Blake smiled.

"Anyway," I continued, "you've met my father. It seems to be in the blood."

We drove on in silence.

Two hours later, I pulled the Jeep over to the side of the track. Greatrex did the same with the Land Rover . We had traveled most of the way down the mountain range and the road was becoming easier. That meant we could gain some speed.

I walked to the Land Rover and opened the rear door. Unexpectedly, Jumaa's face smiled back at me. I'd assumed he would be unconscious.

"Salima is an excellent nurse," he announced. "She has stopped most of the bleeding. I have been out for about an hour and a half but am feeling better now."

Salima spoke in haltering English. "Despite my foolish husband's words, he needs blood soon. The bullet must come out and the wound cleaned if we are to avoid infection."

Jefferson Blake appeared behind me. "Would the hospital in Wadi Halfa be adequate?"

"Yes, sir, it would," she responded.

"Jumaa, how long will it take us to get there?" I asked.

"The journey should take several hours. I'll be fine, but we must be cautious."

"In what way?" asked Blake.

"*Al Fahad* will have sympathizers all over this area. Some civilian, and I fear to add, some in the government. We cannot trust anybody, no matter what uniform they wear."

Jumaa painted a bleak picture. We must rely on ourselves until we make it out of Sudan.

I walked back to the Jeep where Greatrex was attending to the women and children.

"We have a surprise," he said, pointing at one passenger, whose face was partially covered by a blanket.

As the rug was cast aside, the features that emerged were male.

"What in God's name…" I began. As I spoke, I reached into the front seat for my gun.

131

"No, no, not what you think, Nicholas. This is Salah Bahri. The young lady next to him is his daughter, Thiyiba."

The man and the girl both looked up and smiled.

"In a sick twist," Greatrex continued, "it was Salah's wife who was taken by the Shararaa while he was held hostage with the women. He doesn't know where she's gone, but says the terrorists were explicit in saying they needed a female, despite Salah offering to go in her place."

"Let's store that information and move on," I said, masking my surprise. "Jack, will you be able to get a signal here?"

In a moment of genius, Greatrex had discovered a long-range satellite communications system in the terrorist's armory. He'd confiscated it.

"I'll give it my best shot," he replied. "The top of that outcrop looks good," he said, pointing at a bunch of rock around fifty yards north. "I'll wave if I get a signal."

As Greatrex moved off, Vice President Blake came over. "I can't just call up and say 'Jefferson Blake here.' No one would believe me, no matter what code word I used. Do you have someone reliable in Washington you communicate with?"

"Yes, sir, you could say that. Our man on the street is retired Marine General Devlin-Waters."

"My God, Colin!"

"You know him?"

"Know him? He saved my life in Iraq."

"Well, he may be about to do it again, sir."

Fifteen minutes later, Greatrex waved from the top of the rocks. I made my way up to him.

"The General is coming online."

I grabbed the bulky headset from the big fella and waited. It took three minutes before I heard the familiar voice of our former leader.

"Nicholas?"

"General."

"Do you have Blake?" Straight to the point.

"Yes, sir."

"Thank God. Now listen carefully. There've been some developments."

Ten minutes later, we'd made it back down to the road. I had no idea what I would say, or exactly how I would say it.

After making sure Jumaa was all right, I motioned for the big fella and Jefferson Blake to step to one side.

"Okay," I began. "There's a lot of news. First, we will need to make our way into Egypt for our military to extract us. The Chinese are still blowing hot about crossing their air blockade, and no one at the Pentagon has the wherewithal to take them on in the present circumstances. Temporary travel papers are being drawn up in fictitious names for our charges," I nodded toward the families.

For the first time, these people might be able to allow themselves a little hope.

Jefferson Blake interrupted my thoughts. "What do you mean by 'in the present circumstances', Nicholas?"

There was no fooling this man, not even for a second.

"Well, I'm unsure how to say this, sir, but I have some tragic news."

I paused, but there was no way around it.

"I've been informed that two hours ago President Carlton died of a massive heart attack."

"Oh my God," said Blake.

"Shit," said Greatrex.

"The media has just been told. They've also been informed

that the vice president is in transit from Sudan."

Silence.

"So," I looked at Jack Greatrex as I spoke. "I may as well spell this out. We are in hostile foreign territory being pursued by very pissed terrorists while being charged with the safety and extraction of twenty innocent Sudanese civilians and…" I could hardly get through the words… "the president of the United States of America."

"Shit," said Blake.

Chapter 20

Several hours later, our exhausted convoy hit the outskirts of Wadi Halfa, the small town appearing like a mirage rising above the desert sands. The buildings were predominantly single story and made from mud, stone, and brick, and there wasn't a blade of grass in sight. The only respite from the dirt roads and sand dunes was the calming waters of Lake Nubia on our left as we turned onto what appeared to be some sort of main street.

I pulled the Jeep over; Greatrex did the same with the Land Rover. A few locals watched on, their curiosity piqued. The big fella joined me as I opened the Land Rover's back door for what I hoped was the last time to check on Jumaa.

Our Sudanese friend seemed drained. His eyes were half closed, and his breathing labored. There was no question of him being able to complete the journey out of Sudan with us.

"I'll be all right," he said, pausing for a breath every couple of words. "Salima will guide you to the hospital. They'll do what they need to. Do not worry."

Five minutes later, we stopped outside Wadi Halfa's one and only hospital and wondered if we had made the correct decision. The building was compact and looked run-down.

"Stay here," I instructed Vice—no—President Blake. We

needed to keep him from view as much as possible. Every wacko with a grudge against the US government would have seen his face on television or social media over the last few hours, and Greatrex and I weren't the Secret Service.

The spartan cleanliness of the facility surprised me as I walked through the front doors.

A tall man with broad shoulders wearing medical scrubs and a stethoscope around his neck appeared out of a side door.

"Mr. Sharp, I presume. I'm Dr. Mageed. We've been expecting you."

His knowing my name startled me, but I wasn't unduly worried.

"Expecting us?"

Slow on the uptake. I should be doing better than this.

"Yes, sir. We received notification by email of your arrival with a party of around twenty women and children. We are also preparing for a patient with a significant leg wound."

"Who gave you this information?" I asked.

"I'm sorry, Mr. Sharp, I should have mentioned that. Our email came from a Mr. Devlin-Waters in Virginia, along with a deposit of a substantial donation to our hospital account. If I didn't know better, I would say it was hush money."

"Do you know better, Dr. Mageed?"

"It turns out the longer I live, the less I seem to know," replied the smiling doctor. "Now let's get our patient some treatment."

The doctor came out to the Nissan with me and together we manhandled Jumaa inside.

"We'll take him directly to the operating room. We can only provide very primitive facilities here, Mr. Sharp, but they are effective enough."

I nodded as we carried Jumaa the length of the corridor.

A nurse, standing tall and straight in a spotless uniform, appeared out of the operating theater doors just as we reached them.

"This is Nurse Shahid," said the doctor. "She will assist me. I've given the rest of our small staff the remainder of today and tomorrow off. We don't need any town gossip spreading needless rumors."

This medic was on top of everything.

"Now please, Mr. Sharp, allow us to get to work while you bring your friends inside. There is food and water in our hospital kitchen across the corridor. I will give everybody a once over when we are done with Mr. Al Fadil here."

Dr. Mageed's calm demeanor was impressive, as was General Devlin-Waters' ability to probe every corner of the world. Then again, in the eyes of the US government, there was a lot at stake.

Three hours later, Jumaa had been patched up and everyone had eaten. Dr. Mageed had performed a brief health check on all the women and children. He also checked our surprise adult male rescue, Salah. They were all under nourished but should recover well with some rest and good diet. The doctor had tried to examine Jack Greatrex and me, but we insisted there was no need.

It became more interesting when it came to President Blake. Blake had been badly beaten in his time at the terrorist camp, and we couldn't afford for any of his wounds to become infected. He was a robust man, but infection can take the best of us.

The president was in a fair amount of pain but remained stoic as the doctor treated him.

Fortunately, Dr. Mageed showed no sign of recognizing his patient.

It was around 9 p.m. when all finally sat down for the evening.

"What are your plans from here?" asked the doctor, guiding me off into a corner.

"We'd like to get across the border to Egypt either tonight or tomorrow," I replied. "We have friends there who will take care of the rest."

"Your injured friend with the bullet wound cannot travel, at least not for two or three days."

"I understand that." I paused and looked at Dr. Mageed. "Are you able to look after him here?"

"Medically, yes, of course. But I feel he may also need some level of protection. Guns don't fire themselves, Mr. Sharp." The doctor studied me, as if deciding how deep to dig. "I think I have a fair idea where you are going, but tell me, Nicholas, who are you running from?"

"The Shararaa," I replied. There was no point hiding the truth.

There was a sharp intake of breath. "The Shararaa are wicked people. Atha Riek is an evil man."

"Not anymore," I replied. "He's dead."

The doctor looked surprised but took the information in his stride. "As a medical professional, I wish death to no man, but here, I will make an exception. That is good news. You do realize that *Riek's* death won't put an end to the Shararaa?"

"I do, but it will slow them down."

The doctor's face grew weary, and his cheeks sagged as he exhaled loudly. "If possible, it's best you flee before the Shararaa arrive in Wadi Halfa. If they find you here, they'll kill us all."

"What if they find out you helped us or treated our friend?" I asked.

"We'll cross that bridge when we come to it. If need be, my nurse and I will leave. We may apply to the United States for fast-tracked refugee status." He looked across the room at Jefferson Blake, who was watching Greatrex blow shapes out of surgical gloves to amuse the kids.

"Do you think our application would be successful?" he asked, smiling.

"There is no doubt."

"Now, back to planning. I'll arrange to cover your friend's security for a few days. I have family who will help. Regarding your escape, you won't make it out of the country tonight. There are too many patrols. My suggestion is you take tomorrow's ferry. Do you have papers?"

"No, but I'm expecting some to arrive."

"Ah, the email."

"How are you able to receive email communication when the rest of the country is incommunicado?" I asked.

"We are near enough to the border to piggyback off the Egyptian servers when required. Speaking of which, there was another attachment to the email that informed us of your arrival. I didn't open it."

We both stood up. The doctor led me into his small office. He clicked twice on his mouse and the printer in the corner started reeling off sheets. I strode over to look.

First up, there were temporary US travel papers for every member of our party. Then came the surprising part, similar papers in the same names, except they appeared to be official Sudanese travel documents.

How the hell did the general pull that one off?

It was well after 11 p.m. I stared across the hospital waiting room we'd made our temporary home. Some children were sleeping, others were just curled up in their mothers' arms. I couldn't imagine how these traumatic events would affect the rest of their lives.

Greatrex was sitting on the floor next to me. He'd been great with the youngsters, joking, teasing, supporting as required. Greatrex and kids? Who would have thought? I supposed there should have been no surprise given the humanity of the man.

Most of the adults were either gazing into nowhere or whispering to each other. Jumaa's wife and son were with him in his room. The operation to remove the bullet had gone well. Our friend was out of danger but remained weak from blood loss. I didn't want to leave him behind, but I couldn't see any other option. We had to get the families and Blake out of the reach of the Shararaa as soon as possible.

Jefferson Blake had been talking to the doctor out in the corridor. He walked over and perched against the wall next to me.

"I'm worried about these folks," he said.

Most men in his position would be contemplating their return home, anticipating their ascension into the most powerful role on earth. Then again, most men wouldn't be in his position.

"I'm with you on that one," I replied, "but I'm confident that if we make it across the border into Egypt, the extraction will work."

"I understand that," he responded. "The problem lies with

reuniting the families. While the men—or in Salah's case, the woman—don't commit a crime in any foreign country, including our own, I can protect them. If they move ahead with the plans that Atha Riek had arranged, the ball game changes."

"Even considering the circumstances?" asked Greatrex.

"They may be blackmailed into this, but murder is still murder. Nothing will change that."

"Well then, we need to stop these people before they sing from the Shararaa's song sheet," I said.

"Any ideas?" asked Greatrex.

"Maybe, but it's so blindingly simple it might not work."

"Speak up, Nicholas," demanded the president.

"Sudan has been ravaged by violence for years. The previous government was unforgiving in their intolerance, particularly in the south with the horrifying conflict in Darfur. Accordingly, many Sudanese have sought refuge around the world. They're in Canada, Australia, Europe, the US, everywhere that had a big enough heart to take them."

"What are you getting at?" asked Blake.

"It's got me thinking," I said. "Although I've not been here long, it's been easy to see that the Sudanese—bar the occasional terrorist—possess an overwhelming sense of family, including extended family. In today's climate of social media, there is an opportunity. If you look at it the right way, the Sudanese refugees scattered around the world are in fact an enormous underground communications network."

"So, we need to take advantage of that network?"

"Yes. We saw how technologically adept Jumaa's sister, Awadia, was in Khartoum. Social media is not just the privilege of the West, however much we might like to believe it so. Let's get our families online. If they exploit every app and platform available to them to communicate the fact they are out of Sudan and free, their people, including our reluctant terrorist envoys, will get the message.

Blake considered my words, his face drawn tight in contemplation. "It gives us a chance," he replied. "It gives the families a chance."

"We need to get them online tonight. Atha Riek led us to believe his people were moving into place as he spoke," added Greatrex.

"I'll speak to the doctor regarding what computers and devices the hospital has at its disposal," offered Blake.

"Nick and I will talk to the women and Salah," said Greatrex.

It was time to bring our misguided warriors home. Our little online Dunkirk had begun.

Chapter 21

I woke to the morning sun streaming in through the waiting-room windows and the sound of women and children crying.

"What's happened?" I said to Greatrex, standing a few feet away, comforting one of the Sudanese mothers.

"It's all right," he replied. "About half the women received responses from their loved ones, either directly or secondhand through family members. These are good tears, Nicholas, tears of relief."

As I glanced around the room, it became easy to see those who celebrated and those who stayed silent in anguished anticipation. Greatrex looked exhausted. He had been in charge of proceedings. Blake slept on the floor near the door.

"Get some rest, Jack," I told my friend. "The ferry doesn't leave until four this afternoon. We've got plenty of time."

He didn't need persuading.

I left the waiting area and walked down to Jumaa's room. Awake and sitting up, he looked much better. Salima and Ibrahim sat at his bedside. They appeared exhausted, but their smiles spoke of relief.

"Yes, I'm greatly improved, thank you, Nicholas," he answered before I could even ask the question. "The doctor says that if I stay here for twenty-four hours, I'll be all right to travel."

"He said forty-eight hours," interrupted Salima.

"Twenty-four will do it. I don't think I should impose on the good doctor any more than needed." He patted his wife on the hand. She frowned in frustration but didn't argue. "Now, Nicholas, we've been talking," Jumaa's voice took a serious tone. "Although she doesn't want to, Salima has agreed that she and Ibrahim should travel with you into Egypt."

I glanced down at Salima. She looked less than happy.

"It has been too long, many, many months without this stubborn man by my side. I do not wish to leave him, but for the sake of Ibrahim I will go. Jumaa better follow straightaway or I'll come back to get him," she added.

Wise and caring woman.

I looked at Jumaa; I suspected he wasn't as well as he'd made out. This man had given so much to reunite with his family, only to watch them leave again. He had also risked a lot, everything in fact, to help us. He was a genuine patriot and cared deeply for his country and its people.

"Jumaa, will you be all right with leaving your homeland?" I asked.

My friend looked up at me. A deep sadness flooded his watery eyes.

"I have feared the loss of my family," he said as he turned to look at Salima and Ibrahim, his eyes widening, the warmth returning. "I won't relive that hell again. After what I've done to the Shararaa, there will be a price on my head. Maybe more than just my head." He obviously didn't want to say more in front of his son. "I'll continue to work for my country, but from afar. In my heart I know that one day we will all return."

"I may be able to help with that," said Jefferson Blake as he walked up behind me. "How would you feel about a position as the president's special advisor on Sudan?"

Jumaa looked up, his jaw dropping in surprise. "Thank you, Mr. President. I gratefully accept." He turned to Salima. "I think, my love, we will own a big American car." He tried to laugh, but the pain caught him.

"Just make sure you get over that border ASAP, so you live long enough to drive it." I added.

A cool breeze blew off the water, providing us with some relief as we stood on the ferry wharf. The large, once white ship appeared to be over one hundred and fifty feet, bow to stern. Four cranes rode high on its top deck, accompanied by a few lifeboats and plenty of open space. Beyond the vessel, the blue waters of Lake Nubia provided a calming contrast to the desert that surrounded them.

We had been fortunate that the ferry would sail the day after we arrived in Wadi Halfa. It would be seven days until the next sailing. For a population so small, the activity around the boat's departure appeared frantic. Then again, Wadi Halfa had become the major gateway from Sudan to Egypt.

Two of the women purchased our tickets earlier in the day. They used money provided to the hospital through the general's 'generous' donation. Our cover story explained the journey as a community-based single-parents group from Khartoum taking the children on a visit to Cairo. Sadly, because of so much conflict, over so many years, there were a lot of single parents in Sudan. But if things went pear-shaped, we had little evidence to support our deception. Any halfway thorough investigation would expose us. Jefferson Blake now wore the traditional jalabiya, giving him the look of a local.

His dark skin helped in the disguise.

The only explanation we could muster for Greatrex and I cast us as security personnel hired by the travel company who had arranged the tour. It was thinner than a crisp.

We said our goodbyes to Jumaa and Nurse Shahid at the hospital. Having disposed of our vehicles earlier in separate locations—the Land Rover close enough should Jumaa need it—the doctor had then shuttled everyone the short distance to the ferry wharf in his four-wheel drive; hiding in plain sight.

The papers provided by the general had got us through a very relaxed customs process at the wharf. We paid departure tax for everyone. I wondered if we had paid a little over the going rate. It worried me that we had to leave our weapons behind, but we couldn't afford the risk of having several Kalashnikovs and knives found in our possession. As it turned out, our baggage passed through unsearched.

A level of excitement spread among the children as we ushered them onboard. We had booked second-class passage on the deck—that's what a community group would have done—but we also reserved two first-class cabins. They each had a power point and some privacy so we could maintain our social media onslaught. Two thirds of Atha Riek's reluctant envoys had now been back in contact with their wives. Doubtless, some elements of the Shararaa would also monitor social media, even if in a haphazard manner. That our families had lied, stating they had already left Sudan, would throw any determined terrorists off our trail... We hoped.

Greatrex and I stood on the upper foredeck as the ship cast off. My relief grew as the gap of blue water between us and the wharf widened.

"Twenty-four hours until we make Aswan," I announced.

146

"Hmph," came the response.

"What's wrong?"

"Probably just my inbuilt pessimism," admitted the big fella.

"Go on."

"Well, we've been very fortunate since we arrived in Wadi Halfa," he said. "It just plays out a little too much like a happy ending coming too soon."

"I agree that we are nowhere near out of the woods—or should I say, desert—yet," I responded. "Despite the fatigue, we need to stay alert. From what Jumaa has told us, the Shararaa have tentacles that reach everywhere. I'll rest when we are all on US soil."

Greatrex nodded.

With that, the waters of the Nile flowed gently under our feet.

Two hours later, the sun set across the desert horizon. It sent a bold and majestic glow across the waters as we edged our way north. Greatrex and I had checked on the families' welfare and intended to grab some food when Jefferson Blake appeared behind us.

"Sir, I think its best you spend the trip in the cabin," I said.

"Your picture will be all over the media as we head further out of the Sudanese electronic blackout. You're too recognizable," added Greatrex.

"I know, point taken," responded Blake. "The truth is, I was going stir-crazy down there. Besides, I wanted to chat with you two."

"Yes, sir," I replied.

"The moment we set foot on Egyptian soil, our people will be there. At that point, everything changes. I fear they'll build a protective wall around me—it's the nature of the job."

Greatrex and I both nodded.

"Before that happens, I want to say thank you to you both."

I started to speak, but Blake put up his hand.

"Don't even begin with the 'it was nothing' speech," he continued. "You two could have turned your back on this whole situation and waited your time out in Khartoum until things resolved. But you didn't. You risked everything to get me out, not to mention helping those poor, innocent families. I—we—owe you big-time."

"You don't owe us, Mr. President. After fighting beside you as we broke out of the terrorist's camp and watching you stand up for those parents and children, I'm certain you'd have done the same thing in our position."

Blake remained silent.

"If you don't mind me asking, sir, how does it feel knowing you are stepping back into the Western world as the number one man?" Greatrex had never been never comfortable with thanks; changing the subject was his workaround.

"I can tell you this was never my plan. I only came on board as vice president with the proviso that it would be a one-term thing. Some heavy hitters in the party, who I respected, made a persuasive case. His heart problem didn't seem a consideration at the time."

"So, you didn't sign up because of President Carlton?" I asked, probably stepping over the line.

Blake hesitated for a moment. "I shouldn't really say this, but no. I stepped up *despite* Carlton and what he stood for. Please keep that to yourselves."

"Well, now you don't have anyone else to answer to, you can do things your own way, Mr. President," said Greatrex.

Blake turned away from us, staring out over the water toward the darkening horizon. "Yes, I suppose I can operate more independently now, but I disagree with you, Jack. I still have a boss, in fact I have around three hundred and twenty-eight million bosses."

Greatrex looked suitably humbled.

"Not only that," continued Blake, "I'm accountable to every serviceman who defends our democracy. In particular, I'll work for the families of those Secret Service agents and US Air Force personnel who lost their lives in the last few days trying to protect me. I will be their president."

The three of us remained silent for several minutes, listening to the sound of water splashing on the boat's hull.

"Sorry to get so serious," said the president. He then let out a slight chuckle.

"What is it, sir?" I asked.

"I was just thinking, Nicholas, about the offer to share a return ride to the States with you, back at the hotel in Khartoum."

I nodded.

"Who would have thought the ride would end up being a sail down the Nile in a rusty old ferry."

After the laughter, the silence soon returned. I looked out into what had now become a windless desert night. We remained far from home with a long way to go. At the edges of these borders, hidden among the righteous communities of Sudan and Egypt, lurked some terrible people. They would do anything to get their hands on the president of the United States. Right at the moment, our leader was vulnerable, traveling with only two unarmed men to protect him on a journey through a hot bed of volatility.

I knew with certainty the Shararaa, and those like them, wouldn't stop. I also knew they wouldn't hesitate to kill twenty innocent children and their families to get their man. Our man.

I just stared out into the darkness. They were out there somewhere. I could feel it.

Chapter 22

They came two hours later.

I was prowling the lower deck, lost in my own thoughts, when I heard the engines. At least two outboards, possibly more. I moved toward the stern of the ship. Through the darkness, I saw two lots of white foam forming V-shapes around two small craft. They traveled at speed, engines straining. A crewman materialized next to me as I peered out over the railing.

"Is this normal?" I asked him.

"No, it's too early," he said in faltering English. "The Egyptian authorities usually come later. They board and then process people. We are still in Sudanese waters."

Still in Sudanese waters.

Out of nowhere, Greatrex appeared.

"Trouble?"

"Maybe. Make sure Blake stays in his cabin. Also, see if you can get Salah to throw on Blake's civilian clothes. They are about the same size."

He looked perplexed for a moment and then nodded.

Three minutes later, the two rigid-hull inflatable boats pulled up on either side of the ferry. Ninety seconds after that, uniformed Sudanese Armed Forces personnel swarmed over the ferry's rear deck. Their drawn faces and aggressive stances matched the automatic weapons they held tight.

One group of three men made their way up to the bridge. A second group disappeared downstairs. The others spread out along the deck.

"Papers, travel documents, please," they asked to no one in particular.

I edged my way toward the bridge. Before I made it within ten feet, I heard men arguing. Most of the discourse was in Arabic, but from what I figured, the ferry captain wasn't too happy about having his boat boarded.

I wanted to check on Blake, but I didn't want to attract attention to him. Before I'd developed a plan, a young soldier appeared next to me.

"*Yella! Awaraag wa mustana datat al safr!*" he half yelled, his nerves clearly taut.

"Sorry, I only speak English." Nicholas Sharp: calm and collected.

"Your papers and travel documents," he repeated in English, pointing his rifle toward the rear deck where his commanding officer had begun checking everyone's documentation.

I made out I needed to get them from my cabin even though I had them in my pocket, and so I made my way down the cramped space, noting the palpable feeling of alarm. The mothers and children in our group bunched together, exchanging nervous whispers.

Bravado seemed to be the best tactic. I walked straight up to the soldier with the most decorations on his uniform. "I assume you are the commanding officer here. My name is Hayes." I continued speaking before he uttered a word. "My colleague and I have been entrusted with the safety of this

152

group. We've traveled from Khartoum. Here are our papers." I concluded by thrusting our documents in his face.

The officer looked surprised at my aggression, clearly accustomed to people being deferential around him.

"I speak English, Mr. … er… Hayes," he said, grabbing the papers. For five minutes he looked carefully through each set of papers.

"These are only temporary papers," he said. "Where are the originals?"

"We lost them in Khartoum the night before we left. I suppose you're aware there was a coup, riots in the streets. The courier carrying our passports and original documents was mugged and our papers stolen."

"And you could get temporary papers straight away?"

"It took twenty-four hours. I have a friend who is well placed in the bureaucracy. He was able to help," I replied.

The soldier looked me up and down, the half-smile on his lips expressing his amusement. "How very fortunate," he said. "Now you have two other Americans traveling with you," he looked down at the papers. "Mr. Scott?"

On cue, Greatrex stepped forward out of the shadows. Again, the SAF man gave him a once over, without saying a word.

"And Mr. Carter?" Greatrex had cued Salah Bahri to arrive on deck just after him. He wore Jefferson Blake's Western clothes.

"You are Carter?"

Salah nodded.

"You look very African to me," said the soldier.

"Yes, sir, I originally came from Sudan. I have lived in America for several years. Carter is now my legal name." The slight American inflection that Salah pulled off was impressive. Perhaps all Sudanese are actors.

The officer issued instructions to an offsider who rounded up our families. Three other soldiers spread out, surrounding them.

"Count them," said the officer. "There should be ten children, nine women and one man." Speaking in English, it was clear the lead man wanted us to understand his orders.

After counting heads, the soldier walked back to his commander and spoke to him in Sudanese. The officer paused before glancing up at me.

"There are ten children and nine women. There is a male missing. Please explain this?"

Everyone remained silent, eyes locked on me. The only sound, the throb of the ferry's engines as the ship meandered forward.

I looked across the deck. The focused expressions on the soldiers' faces suggested this was no routine inspection.

"Answer me now, Mr. Hayes, or we shall have to turn this ferry about and return to Wadi Halfa until we sort this matter."

"That man never boarded the boat," I said. "He took ill with a fever at the wharf. He returned to town to seek medical attention." It was a risk. If the soldiers went to the hospital to check, I hoped our doctor would back us up. "In the confusion, he must have forgotten to take his papers."

The officer hesitated. A small seed of doubt planted.

"One moment please."

The soldier surprised me by strutting over to the railing and calling down into the darkness. I edged over to get a look. Two men in robes perched in one inflatable. Each had a Kalashnikov sitting on his lap.

There was a heated exchange between the men and the officer, the latter seeming under duress.

The women and children clasped each other, wide-eyed and terrified. There was nothing I could do to help them.

At that moment, the ship's captain came barreling down to the rear deck. He addressed the officer in English.

"I direct you to leave my vessel immediately. In less than a minute, we'll enter Egyptian waters where you have no authority. Unless you wish to create an international incident and all the ramifications that go with it, I suggest you go now!"

"Then stop the boat," yelled the officer.

"You idiot—even if I turned the engines off straightaway, we would drift into Egyptian waters before we could turn about. The Egyptian authorities know we are here. I spoke to them as soon as I noticed you approaching us." Hell hath no fury like a ship's master whose authority has been questioned.

The Sudanese officer hesitated for half a moment more before turning to me, his eyes blazing. Fear or anger, it was hard to read.

"Get all the men back on the boats… now. We're going." His offsider obeyed.

Ninety seconds later, the decks clear of soldiers, our group melted into a sigh of collective relief.

Too soon.

Just before the inflatables pushed off, two pairs of weathered hands grappled the side rail. The two robed Sudanese who had been sitting alongside vaulted over the balustrade.

Before Greatrex or I reacted, each of them had a gun pointed directly at us.

"Mr. Sharp, Mr. Greatrex, you will take us to President Blake right now, please."

155

To make his point, the speaker swiveled his weapon, aimed it across the deck at one of the crewmen, and gunned him down in a burst of automatic fire.

We'd been so close.

Chapter 23

They pushed us along the starboard deck, toward the bow. The armed men stood far enough back that we couldn't disarm them and close enough that they could gun us down if we tried anything. I stopped when we reached the stairwell that led down to Blake's cabin.

"I don't know who you are," I said, "but this is a complete waste of time. I told the soldier that the man—"

"Just shut up, Sharp. Do you think we are stupid? You have murdered Atha Riek and killed too many of our brothers. The only reason you are alive now is to hand over your president."

Straight to the point.

Halfway down the stairs, one terrorist lunged forward. For a split second, I figured he'd moved to assault me, but the surprised look on his face told a different story.

I stepped aside and shoved the man passed me, letting gravity do its thing. As he fell, I pressed myself against the wall, bracing for the slugs from his comrade's Kalashnikov to tear through the enclosed space, but it didn't happen.

At the top of the stairs the other man stood gasping for breath. The cause of his discomfort was a large forearm around his neck; muscles tensed, squeezing his throat like a python crushing its prey. By the time I picked up his dropped weapon, the terrorist had gone limp.

The arm pulled back and the terrorist's body fell away. In his place stood President Jefferson Blake.

"I told you I'd been going stir-crazy down there," he said.

At that moment the ferry's captain came bustling around the corner. He paused when he saw the dead terrorists.

"Well, that's that then," he announced.

"It was very fortunate, Captain," I began, "that we were entering Egyptian waters. Without you pointing that out, we would have been in a lot of trouble."

"What do you mean?" he responded, a smile creeping onto his face. "We don't enter Egyptian territory for another twenty minutes."

Thank God for angry sailors.

After we'd disposed of the terrorists' bodies over the side, Blake, Greatrex and I gulped down a warm cup of coffee with our newfound friend, Captain Mahir. The captain had assured us ten minutes previously that we were now really in Egyptian waters. The relief for everyone, including our fleeing families, was immense.

Captain Mahir had left us in no doubt about his attitude toward authorities bullying desperate refugees.

"These days I'm just a ferry skipper," he said, shrugging his shoulders. "My wife prefers me closer to home as we enter our dotage. Sadly, in my thirty years at sea, I've seen too many unpleasant situations where war mongers rule at the point of a gun. The arrogance of those soldiers boarding my vessel was intolerable."

We were glad for his intolerance.

The words had barely left his mouth when our world lit up.

Night turned into day as an arc of bright lights blazed across the length of the ship. We swiveled to get a look. At least six rigid-hull inflatable boats, similar to the ones used by the Sudanese soldiers, surrounded the vessel. The one difference: they had access to modern, *silent*-running outboards.

The captain reached toward the throttle. "We can't outrun them, but we can make it harder for them to board."

I placed my hand on his arm. "I would wait, Captain. This may not be what you think."

Within two minutes, all the ship's decks were swarming with military personnel in Egyptian uniforms.

"What the hell?" said the captain. "The authorities from Cairo usually send one craft with just a couple of men to process our passengers."

At that point a soldier, high-ranking, judging from his uniform, stormed onto the bridge. Four armed soldiers accompanied him.

He addressed the skipper. "Captain, I am Major Gamal from the Egyptian Special Forces Unit 777. I command you to halt your vessel, immediately."

"Like hell," replied the skipper, his voice peaking in anger.

It was time to defuse the situation, the voice of reason. "Before things get out of hand, Captain, I should explain something about our human cargo."

Five minutes later, with our captain in shock about his VIP passenger, we listened to a terse conversation between Jefferson Blake and the Egyptian officer.

"Mr. President, sir, I have explicit orders to transfer you, Mr. Sharp, and Mr. Greatrex off the vessel now. Your refugee friends are to continue their journey and go through the

159

usual immigration process, albeit fast-tracked, considering the circumstances."

"With all due respect," replied Jefferson Blake, "I don't care what your orders say, Major, I am not leaving this ship without the entire contingent of people I boarded with."

"But, sir, my instructions…"

"You'd better contact your superiors and tell them you're unable to extricate the president of the United States and had to leave him in transit with terrorists in pursuit."

Greatrex and I shared a grin. With every passing minute, President Jefferson Blake was growing in my estimation.

Blake walked over to the edge of the bridge and looked over the side of the ship. "You have brought enough small craft to carry everyone, although it may entail leaving a few soldiers behind."

"Mr. President, we need the soldiers to guard and transport you."

"Not if I'm not going."

The major was outclassed.

His shoulders sagged as he collapsed in defeat. "One moment, please, sir—I will make a call." With that, he disappeared back onto the rear deck.

Three minutes later, we could hear orders being barked across the deck. The officer returned to the bridge.

"It would be my honor, sir, to escort you, your two colleagues and the rest of your party to our boats. As we speak, transportation arrangements are being made for all of you for an extended journey."

Deal done.

The next few hours were a morass of activity and movement.

When the US government kick in, they kick in big-time. So do their allies. No chances were being taken in extracting the US president from a volatile situation.

A fleet of four-wheel drives waited for us on the riverbanks. We drove a few miles to a flat and remote location. Right on cue, two American Pave Hawks appeared from above. The Egyptian troops ushered our party onboard, just before the choppers fled upward, into the darkened sky.

Tiran Island hosts a Multinational Force and Observers peacekeeping force, overseeing implementation of the peace treaty between Egypt and Israel. The US is part of that force. We alighted the helicopters into the warm night air as we waited there for our final ride to arrive.

Making the most of the brief time we had, we used the MFO communications office to check on the fate of the family members sent abroad by the Shararaa. All but one had made contact through our social network campaign.

"Who hasn't established contact?" I asked Greatrex as he sat at a table in a corner of the room checking off names.

Jefferson Blake had begun a debriefing process by US Intelligence elsewhere on the base. As he predicted, a wall of security surrounded him as soon as we arrived in US hands.

"It's Salah Bahri's wife, Sua'd," said Greatrex.

"Damn it."

One of the US communication personnel walked across the room toward us.

"Mr. Sharp?"

"Yes, Officer, what can I do for you?"

"I have a Mr. Al Fadil online for you."

"I'll take it," I said. I'd put in a call to the hospital in Wadi Halfa earlier.

161

The warrant officer led me back past rows of chairs and equipment to a computer station. As I sat down, Jumaa's image appeared on the screen.

"How are you, my friend?" I asked, barely containing my relief at the sight of his smiling face.

"Very well, Nicholas. As this call comes from a military installation, I'm assuming you all made it over the border?"

"Yes, we're all fine. How's your recovery going?"

"All good, but we may have a problem."

"Go on."

"Late last night, I had a visitor at the hospital. It was a Sudanese Armed Forces officer named Akhdhr. He informed me he had boarded your boat, and that there was one man missing from your group. He explained the situation and asked if I was that man."

I hoped Jumaa had covered himself.

"I told him I was."

"Did he question you further, asking for details?

"Well, there is the strange thing. He didn't ask for more information. He didn't check my identification, he didn't even inquire about the nature of my illness. His only concern seemed to be that I'd been with your group."

Considering Jumaa's 'illness' was a bullet wound, that was a relief.

My friend continued. "From there it just becomes more odd. Not only was he not very inquisitive, but at one point, he ordered his two soldiers to leave the room."

I couldn't see where this was going.

Jumaa face drew tight in concentration. "The officer then requested I give you a message, if you were still alive."

"A message?"

"He said to tell you he overheard a conversation between the two 'civilians' on the boat. I hope that means something to you, Nicholas."

"Yes, Jumaa, it does."

"He also asked me to tell you they'd been talking about one key person in their plans. They said that it doesn't matter if they miss getting the US president in Sudan because their agent would get him in Washington."

My head was a maze of possibilities, all bad.

"The thing is," continued Jumaa, "I believe the Sudanese officer had been under some duress from the Shararaa, but wanted to help us. He told me he didn't hear the agent's name, but there was one bit of useful information."

"Yes."

"Apparently, the person they were referring to, perhaps an assassin of some sort, was referred to as 'she.'"

I sat back in my chair. I considered Salah Bahri's wife, who we could not contact. There seemed little chance that was a coincidence. As I reflected further, I realized there was no other plausible explanation. The terrorists had not given up.

The Shararaa were sending Sua'd Bahri to assassinate President Jefferson Blake in Washington, and we had no idea how they were planning to do it.

Chapter 24

Six Weeks Later

Kaitlin Reed's blond hair fell across her face as her blue eyes shot laser beams through my heart.

"It's been a while, Nicholas," she said.

"Much too long, Kaitlin," I responded.

"I heard that you've been busy."

There it was. Kaitlin made her point. She was aware I'd been involved with a woman when I was in Europe a few months back. I assumed the general told her—after all, he was her stepfather. Kaitlin probably gleaned that the situation didn't end well. The woman, Elena, was dead. I'd nearly ended up the same way. I didn't want to talk about it and hoped Kaitlin would find the grace to let it go.

Although the conversation faltered, we were not sitting in silence. Some low-key blues played through the club's sound system as we sipped our wine. For a moment, the tiny table between us seemed like an unfathomable gap.

I looked around the room. We were in a small jazz and blues club down an out-of-the way alley in Georgetown, Washington. Wooden chairs and undersized tables crowded together, black-and-white pictures of jazz greats adorned the industrial brick walls, the atmosphere spelling upmarket bohemian. As we chatted, waiting for the headline act to take the stage, I allowed myself a small grin, pleased that I'd chosen a venue with a built-in distraction as our meeting place.

"It's all right, Nicholas, cut out the 'naughty child caught with his hand in the cookie jar' look. We are both grown-ups."

There was another pause.

"My stepfather told me what happened—I'm just glad you're okay."

This beautiful woman empowered more grace than I deserved.

"I suppose we should talk business," she continued. "The general is out of town and asked me to bring you up to date on the Sudanese situation."

I sat up in my chair, attentive, not to mention relieved that the conversation had turned.

"In the weeks since you returned to the States, there has been no word from the Shararaa. Once the Sudanese government put down the coup and settled back into business, the terrorist group went silent," she said.

"That has to be a positive thing," I responded, "although I don't believe for a second that the Shararaa have given up."

"No, the general doesn't suspect so either. Neither does the United States government. Have you connected with President Blake since you and Jack pulled him out of Sudan?"

"I figure he's been busy setting up shop and calming the people, both within and outside Washington. Jack and I met with him once at Joint Base Andrews. The presidential minders are trying to keep what happened in Sudan very low key, in fact, under-the-radar low key. When we got together for our 'off the record' meeting, the president was very kind with his words of gratitude, considering he helped us just as much as we helped him."

Kaitlin nodded. "Jefferson Blake is a principled man, but he is alone in a swamp of alligators. He hasn't got the political backing of a career politician."

"But he seems to have public support."

"That's why his party tolerates him, although I'm not convinced they understand the depth of his conviction when it comes to morality."

I hadn't heard Kaitlin talk so explicitly about political life in the country's capital before.

"Did the general give you an update on the families that came out with us? I'm in regular communication with Jumaa now that he's here in Washington. However, neither he nor I are aware of the authorities contacting Salah Bahri's wife, Sua'd.

"That's one reason I'm here," said Kaitlin. "None of the official channels of investigation turned up anything. Someone in the government had a quiet word with the general who asked me to speak with you. They hope that with Jumaa's help, you may find out some information though 'informal' channels."

"I doubt it," I replied. "Jumaa has tried everything. Sua'd Bahri has simply disappeared off the map. There's no sign she's even alive."

"Do you think she's alive?" asked Kaitlin.

I considered her question. "Yes, I do, in fact, I'm sure of it. I believe the Shararaa have sent her to ground. My gut tells me they'll make another attempt on President Blake's life, and it will somehow involve Sua'd Bahri."

Before Kaitlin could respond, a voice came over the sound system. "Please welcome to the stage, Lucia Dubois." Thirty seconds into the opening song, the entire room sat entranced by the enchanting young jazz singer sitting at the piano. That left the two of us marooned on our respective islands of thought, with jazz accompaniment. The music was soothing, my thoughts were not.

Forty-five minutes later, the singer and her band took a bow, basking in the warm applause. The audience allowed them to leave the stage, knowing they would be back for a second set.

I was keen to resume my conversation with Kaitlin. There was way too much troubling me about the whole Sudanese thing. I'd hoped that the authorities would have put it all to bed by now. Apparently not. I'd hung around Washington for what I assumed would be a brief time until things settled.

The waitress brought a second bottle of wine to our table. Probably not a brilliant idea on several levels, so I poured us each a glass.

"So, if the Shararaa are lying dormant, what does it mean? Do the authorities figure we caused them a vast setback when we killed Atha Riek, or are the terrorists working on another plan?" I asked.

"That's the question everyone is asking, but no one seems to be able to answer. Nicholas, you said your gut feeling was that they were up to something. Why?" Kaitlin was straight back into business.

"Jumaa made it clear to Jack and me that the Shararaa had tentacles that reached everywhere, both outside and inside the Sudanese government. That became obvious by their influence on the SAF personnel on the ferry. We drove a big dent into their paramilitary operations but would have had only a minor effect on their political ambitions."

"Well then, I've got some information for you that could

shine some light on that. Did Jumaa ever tell you that Atha Riek had a brother?"

I leaned forward in my chair. "No."

"He probably didn't know, very few people do. The general's network did some digging. While there is no official proof that a sibling exists, there were rumors. Riek's father was also a radical Muslim. My stepfather's people located some hospital records that showed that Atha Riek was born six minutes after midnight, October twenty-forth, thirty-one years ago. The strange thing is that the hospital surgical records show another birth recorded to the same doctor seven minutes after that. In itself, that's not unusual. What is odd, however, is that there was no second birth certificate registered that matches the location and time of the two births. The only birth registered was Atha Riek. The second child never officially existed."

I paused for a moment. "It could be a bureaucratic mistake—I'm sure the system in Sudan was not infallible back then. Ours wasn't—there are many stories of mix-ups at birth."

"On its own, maybe so," said Katlin. "It all became more concerning when we realized that not only did Riek's mother die during childbirth, but the attending doctor and nurse both died in separate accidents a short time later."

The colonel's ability to research deep into the past and dig up facts others overlooked had helped him climb the ladder to the top of the military intelligence tree. What he found out here had frightening implications. I let my mind process what I'd just learned.

"Suppose Riek's radical-leaning father had sent the other son away. Is it possible he planned for one sibling to be the violent face of the Shararaa and the other to work quietly behind the scenes, possibly even making his way into government service?"

"It sounds a bit far-fetched," replied Kaitlin. "But, on the other hand, the father was killed ten years later, attempting to blow up a bus full of Christian school children." Across the table, Kaitlin sank back into her chair, tilting her head to one side. She closed her eyes and sighed. "Is it really possible for someone to plan and commit such wickedness?"

I put my elbows on the table, pressed my mouth into my hands and gazed into nowhere. Kaitlin and the noisy club faded away. I was back in the mountains of Batn-El-Hajar, smelling the warm, dry air and feeling the sand and stone under my feet. The cold, empty gaze of Atha Riek's lifeless eyes penetrated me. I had stared through the hole in his soul, where any empathy or decency should exist, as he prepared to slaughter those women and children.

"Yes, Kaitlin, such evil does exist… I've seen it up close." I'd returned to the room. "If what you are telling me is true, we are in deep shit. No one, and I mean no one, will be able to guarantee President Blake's safety. These people are smart and well resourced. They've got through the Secret Service before, they'll do it again."

I stood up, kissed Kaitlin on the cheek, left some money for the bill and turned to leave.

"Where are you going, Nicholas?"

"I'm going to find Greatrex and Jumaa. We've worked outside the system before, we can do it again. It's the only way to stop this."

"Not this time, buddy!" announced Kaitlin. "I'm coming too."

I could tell from her piercing blue eyes and crinkled brow that there was no stopping her. The general's stubborn influence radiated off her face. I reached down, took her hand and led her to the door, suddenly feeling very sober.

Chapter 25

"My stepfather is flying in tonight," said Kaitlin as she hung up the phone.

We sat in the lounge room of the grand house on the general's expansive estate in Maryland. I glanced at Greatrex, sprawled across a very expensive-looking sofa. To my right, Jumaa perched upright and attentive on a leather Chesterfield chair. He had only arrived a short time ago. We had just updated him on the discussion that Kaitlin and I had the night before at the jazz club. I'd phoned Greatrex back in LA the moment I returned to my hotel in Washington. Lucid but grumbling, he'd caught the red-eye overnight.

"I understand the concern," said the big fella, "but I'm a little uncertain how the three of us can protect Jefferson Blake any more than the entire combined forces of the Secret Service, the FBI and the CIA, to name just a few."

"You are probably right," I replied. "The only thing is, I reckon we left the job half-done. The president is still in danger."

"It is my duty to help if I can," said Jumaa. "Jefferson Blake is an ally to my country—if there's anything I'm able to do to prevent any countrymen of mine harming him, I will do it." As our Sudanese friend spoke, his eyes wandered around the luxurious space and out the enormous windows to the green paddocks beyond. "I'm enjoying my new life here," he added, "although as I look out this window, I seem a long way from my homeland."

"But not in your heart," I said.

"No, not in my heart, especially since Salima, Ibrahim, and I are together again here in the US."

Jumaa got up and paced in front of the fireplace. His bullet wound had healed well. He was one tough individual.

Kaitlin shoved Greatrex's legs off the couch and sat next to him. "There is some more news from my stepfather's contacts. It would appear there has been some intelligence chatter regarding a possible attempt on the president's life. The problem is that we are getting mixed messages."

"What do you mean?" I asked.

"Well, there is some intel regarding a potential assassination of Jefferson Blake, but there is also talk of an attack on the Sudanese president."

"Is there any word on the Shararaa being behind either attempt?" inquired Greatrex.

"There is the confusion," replied Kaitlin. "They have linked the Shararaa to both plots."

Jumaa walked across the room and sat back in his chair. "I fear there may be some logic in the mixed messages," he declared.

Kaitlin looked perplexed.

"You're aware I only started my new role as the special presidential advisor on Sudan a week ago?" he said.

We all nodded.

"The reason they rushed my appointment through was that there is an event being planned."

"What sort of event?" I asked.

"To help calm the unrest in Sudan, and celebrate the Sudanese–US relationship, President Blake has decided to host a state dinner for the Sudanese president. The White House has not yet announced it."

"For the Shararaa, that means two birds with one stone," said Greatrex.

"I understand, what you're saying makes sense," added Kaitlin, "but in what universe can a terrorist group infiltrate the White House?"

"They couldn't," I replied. "But in terms of an official state dinner, there is always a chance they may have some clandestine aid from within the Sudanese government."

"Think this through for a minute," said Greatrex. "If we believe that Salah's wife, Sua'd, is part of this plot, then the Shararaa have a problem. We know what she looks like. No identifiable face will make it through White House security, help or no help."

"And they know that we know that," I replied.

Silence pervaded the room.

"Jumaa," I said, "do you think you can arrange a meeting for us with President Blake?"

"I'm certain he would be glad to see you," replied the new presidential advisor.

"So be it. We need to persuade the president not to go ahead with the dinner before they announce it."

As soon as the words left my mouth, I realized that would never happen.

Chapter 26

I would defy any visitor walking into the Oval Office not to feel in awe. The sense of gravitas and occasion is immense. As Greatrex, Jumaa, and I walked through the door, the brightness of the room struck us; the morning light flooding through the windows behind the president's desk presented a majestic silhouette.

"The president will join you shortly," said the voice of the dark-suited Secret Service agent who had shown us in.

We all gazed around the room, like kids at a theme park. I looked again at the desk. "Is that...?"

"Yes, the Resolute desk," replied the agent. "It was brought back here by President Blake. He felt it was an important part of American history."

"Brought it back?" I asked.

"Yes, not every president has the same sense of tradition. The president's predecessor had the desk stored elsewhere in the White House."

I was wondering if our knowledgeable Secret Service agent had allowed a little disapproval of the former incumbent to show.

"Nicholas, Jack, Jumaa, great to see you." The voice of Jefferson Blake boomed across the room as he entered the office from the garden door. Another agent accompanied him.

"Mr. President, it's once again an honor," I said.

The president waved a hand toward the agent who had been our history teacher. "I see you've met Abe Peterson. Abe is the head of my Secret Service detail. He has been my chief protector since I became vice president, and many more years before that—we served together."

I offered my hand, as did Jack. Jumaa had already met the man.

Peterson glanced at the president, who gave him the slightest nod. "Mr. Sharp and Mr. Greatrex, I owe you my deepest thanks," he said.

"How so?" I asked.

The agent appeared sheepish. It wasn't a disposition that suited him. "When the then vice president was in Sudan, I was on leave. It was the birth of my first grandchild. We planned it before they announced the Sudan trip."

"Abe tried to withdraw his leave application when he heard where I was going. I wouldn't hear of it," interrupted the president.

"I was, in effect, ordered to take time off by the vice president and my wife. I wasn't happy. When Vice President Blake went AWOL, I was downright furious."

"But it all worked out, my old friend," reassured the president.

"Yes, it did, and from what I understand it was thanks to you two," said Peterson, looking at Greatrex and I, "with a fair amount of help from Mr. Al Fadil."

"I wouldn't underestimate the contribution made by our beloved leader," I ventured, while casting a glance at Jefferson

175

Blake.

"Yes, I'm aware just how stubborn he can be," replied Peterson.

We shared a group chuckle. Nicholas Sharp: right at home in the Oval Office.

Blake invited us to take a seat on the pair of elegant couches I'd seen a hundred times on television. Abe Peterson stood next to the door.

"Now, tell me, what can I do for you?" he asked.

I told the president everything we had learned. Greatrex and Jumaa filled in the gaps.

"Suffice to say, Mr. President, it is our unsolicited recommendation that you do not announce, nor hold the state dinner for the president of Sudan until your safety can be assured," I announced.

President Blake looked over to Peterson.

"Sir, I agree with these gentlemen. We'd place you in a position of needless risk if we move forward with our plans," he added.

The agent spoke like an ally, but from his expression I saw that he held little hope.

Jefferson Blake was silent for a few moments. I wasn't sure whether he was considering our request or wondering how to let us down easy.

"The moment a person takes this job," he began, "he or she is agreeing to be at risk. Whoever holds the presidency of the United States automatically becomes one of the most revered figures in the world... and one of the most reviled. I'm a big boy—I was aware of the dangers coming in the door."

"But sir—" interrupted Peterson.

Blake held up his hand. "I know what you will say, Abe, and

I appreciate it. The bottom line, however, is that our friends in Sudan are still going through turmoil. They require our support. The people of our own country need to see we are here and ready to help. I fear that the previous administration may have led Americans to believe that being a moral citizen of the world was not worth the trouble."

The president sat back and considered his words.

"Everyone in this room has made sacrifices to keep me alive," Blake took his time to look all of us in the eye. "I can't tell you how much I appreciate that, but the bottom line is clear in this situation. If you kept me safe for a purpose, it was so I could be a moral leader who doesn't back down under threat. I'm sorry, gentlemen, the visit and the state dinner will proceed."

No one said a word as the weight of the president's words hung in the silence. Those of us that knew the man hadn't expected a different outcome.

"Mr. President, I understand and respect your position. Could I, however, ask you one thing? Would you allow Jack and I not only to be present at the dinner but also to access some government resources so we can hunt around for more information on the Shararaa's plan and Sua'd Bahri's whereabouts?"

Jefferson Blake spoke. "We have the Secret Service, the FBI, the CIA and Homeland Security all working on this, and you two figure you'll find something they missed? What do you make of that, Agent Peterson?"

Across the room, Abe Peterson frowned. "Sir, we are better resourced than any other protection system in the world. Our sole mission is the safety of you, your family and your colleagues. We know our job, Mr. President, and we are trained to do it well." The agent paused for a moment, then a smile crept onto his face. "On the other hand, when you were in Sudan, sir, and in deep strife, it was Mr. Sharp, Mr. Greatrex, and Mr. Al Fadil who got you out. I say bring them on board, sir."

"Done deal. Nicholas, Jack, you're in, and it will be easier than you expect," declared the most powerful man on earth.

Jefferson Blake appeared amused by the bewilderment on our faces. "Well," he said, "the fact is, the Sudanese president has requested that P.D. Bailey and his band perform at the state dinner, so you two will be there, anyway. Jumaa will be there as one of my most trusted advisors on Sudan."

"Are there other performers?" asked Greatrex.

"The Sudanese government is bringing some musicians. I imagine the evening will end up being the exchange of culture that the Shararaa interrupted so devastatingly in Khartoum," said Blake.

"Do you have a date set yet?" I inquired.

"I understand it is to be in three weeks," responded the president.

"That doesn't leave us much time," said Greatrex.

"I have every confidence in you all," replied the president. "I should add that General Devlin-Waters spoke to the Secret Service this morning to update them with your latest information. Nicholas, hearing you speak of the possibility of Atha Riek having a brother tight with the Sudanese government is very concerning. If that intel is true, there is little doubt there will be another attempt to disrupt our democracy and this administration."

"With respect, Mr. President, I think it will be more than that," I said.

"In what way, Nicholas?"

"I believe this has become personal. If there is a brother—and it sounds like there is—I'm certain he will come directly after you."

Blake seemed to be pondering my words. "Personal... You may be right."

The president didn't seem fazed by the idea.

Jumaa interrupted the silence. "Mr. President, can you tell us when you will announce the Sudanese president's visit and the state dinner?"

"Well, about that..." replied the commander-in-chief.

Chapter 27

It was only a few minutes' walk from the Oval Office to the James S. Brady Press Briefing Room.

It took Jack Greatrex and I much longer to make the journey. After we had left President Blake, we spent the best part of two hours with Abe Peterson in a small West Wing office, thrashing out scenarios and exchanging information. It was clear that the president was in expert hands, protected by such a dedicated operator.

During our meeting, Peterson took a phone call. As he listened, his face tightened in concern. "Our sources have now confirmed that Atha Riek had a twin brother, fraternal, not identical," he told us.

"In other words, no one knows what he looks like," I added.

"Exactly," replied the agent. "Insiders close to the Shararaa say both siblings were equally dedicated to their cause. They rarely met in person and all communication remained extremely secretive."

"What a family," said Greatrex, "bound by common hatred."

"I'm going upstairs to tell the president," announced Peterson. "Please remain here."

Blake had invited Greatrex and I to watch the afternoon's press briefing announcing the Sudanese official visit, although he requested we stay out of sight. The president's time in Sudan and his method of extraction had been kept under wraps. News outlets reported that several US personnel had died in an attempt on Blake's life during the coup, but no more.

Jean Staples, the White House press secretary, would run the briefing, but President Blake wanted to announce the Sudanese president's visit and state dinner himself. He wanted to send a message.

When the press secretary walked up to the podium at the front of the small auditorium, members of the White House press pool sat relaxed, business as usual. When she announced, "Ladies and Gentlemen, the President of the United States," the mood suddenly became deferential, ties smoothed, skirts adjusted, backs straight.

"Please, sit down," instructed Blake as the reporters took to their feet after he strode on to the podium. "I've asked Jean to give me a little time here because I'd like to inform you all of an important visit to Washington by the head of a country we hold in the highest and warmest regard. I speak of my good friend, President Sabbir of Sudan."

Jefferson Blake continued his speech, giving a brief history of the relationship between the two countries and praising Sudan's move toward democracy. He spoke briefly about Sabbir's success in crushing the recent coup. Finally, he announced he would take questions.

Hands across the room shot up. Jean Staples managed the journalists like a teacher with a tough class.

"Mr. President. This will be your first official state visit since taking office. Can you tell us about the menu and entertainment for the event?"

Staples shoulders relaxed, she seemed relieved the questions were coming in light.

"My office will make announcements as information is confirmed," said the president. "I can tell you, however, that the Sudanese president has requested that American blues and soul legend P.D. Bailey perform."

"Mr. President, as a widower, can you inform us who'll undertake the first lady's traditional duties?"

Not very subtle.

Blake winced slightly and said, "My daughter Cassandra has offered to help with the arrangements."

Several representatives of the press gallery nodded in approval.

Then from the center of the room, "Mr. President, Tom Saunders, *Washington Post*. There are rumors circulating that your recent extradition from Sudan was difficult and not processed through regular diplomatic and security procedures. Can you elaborate on that, sir?"

Press Secretary Staples spoke before Blake could get a word out. "We will not be addressing rumors in this forum, Tom, you know better than that. Next question."

President Blake showed no reaction as the exchange took place.

"Mr. President, Juliet Bross from the *New York Times*. Sources have told us that a terrorist group in Sudan held you captive. Can you confirm that, please?"

Murmurs echoed across the room. The jackals were becoming emboldened.

"Again, we will not be addressing unsubstantiated rumors," said Staples.

Then from the back corner, a rather weary-looking reporter with the craggy, weather-beaten manner of a veteran scribe stood up, unasked.

"Joe Connors, Mr. President, freelance for *Time* magazine."

"Now, Joe, you'll have to wait…" attempted the press secretary.

The journalist refused to be ignored, and Jean Staples was struggling.

"I don't mean to be disrespectful, Mr. President, but I've just returned from the Batn-El-Hajar region of Sudan. I recorded an interview with an eyewitness who stated that you were actively involved in the death of the terrorist leader, Atha Riek. Can you please confirm that?"

Connor's last words were drowned in the uproar.

"I will call this briefing off if you people can't behave in a civilized—"

"No!" said the booming voice from behind the podium microphone. "I would like to address these insinuations."

The room dropped to an immediate silence. The president of the United States had something to say.

"For the last few weeks, our country has been in mourning. We've mourned the loss of President Carlton, and we've mourned the loss of the brave American personnel who gave their lives to protect not only me but, more importantly, our democratic values. We have grieved together as a community, and we have grieved privately as the friends, families, and colleagues of those lost. For those closest to our fallen heroes, the tears will continue for an unimaginable time. To you all, I offer my thoughts, my prayers, and the support of a grateful nation."

The president paused to look around the room. The collective focus was undivided.

"But you already know thoughts and prayers are not

enough."

Eyebrows raised.

"It was my decision to protect you, the American public, from the details of the events in Sudan. I believed that as a nation we needed time to heal without distraction. That time has now passed."

There wasn't a sound from the journalists. No one wanted to interrupt.

"Now, to the truth… From Khartoum, I was taken by force to the northern Batn-El-Hajar region, in the mountains. They held me in a cave…"

For twenty minutes, the president told his story. By the time the Jefferson Blake was almost done, the most inquisitive, talkative journalists in the world sat in a silent fog of disbelief.

The president offered a brief half-smile. "When you retrieve your ability to speak and write, I urge you to discard your initial instinct to blame this on religious tension. We are better than that. We *must* be better than that. This despicable group hid behind the pretense of religion, but it is not who they were. They were snakes and murderers, men without conscience, and most certainly without justifiable cause. I repeat, it was not Muslim believers who held me captive, it was a small cluster of rancid bullies, traitors to their own county and religion. I ask you to remember that before you pass judgment."

The president stepped back from the microphone for a few quick seconds as the more liberal members of the press nodded in approval.

Then, "Mr. President. You haven't spoken of your escape or the death of Atha Riek?"

"It was my good fortune that two of our own countrymen

plus one brave Sudanese citizen infiltrated the terrorist enclave to rescue me. Please don't ask their names. Like the heroes they are, they wish to remain unidentified. Together, we decided that we wouldn't leave without the hostage families. To do so would have guaranteed their immediate deaths. There was a firefight, and we made it out, all of us."

Whispers rippled across the room.

"You may say that the man before you is a politician, words are easy. I may be in politics now, although that was never my intent, but on that night in Sudan, as we fought to survive and to liberate, I was not a politician. I was an American. I acted with a strength of resolve that I honestly believe most righteous people would in the circumstances.

"Let me be clear in saying that it was that resolve that gave me courage that night. Courage to pull the trigger that ushered Atha Riek from this mortal world."

The room erupted.

The president stood at the podium, motionless, waiting for calm.

"Mr. President, have all the potential bombers been reunited with their families?"

"Almost all. For obvious reasons of security, I cannot give you more information."

Her name.

"I can, however, tell you this. It has recently come to our attention that the Shararaa leader, Riek, had a twin brother. We understand that although not identical twins, the siblings shared the same demonic hatred of democratic values. I'm told the brother, name yet unknown, is equally responsible for my capture and the deaths of our American personnel. We believe he is planning a new attempt on my life and that of

President Sabbir. The president and I have spoken—we both agree that we will not cower in the face of this threat. We will not hide away until the danger is over. The state visit remains on the schedule and will not be postponed."

Jefferson Blake lowered his head for a moment. When he looked up his eyes radiated the strength of steel.

"I have no doubt that Riek's sibling has access to this press conference, so I'll now address my comments directly to him.

"We don't know your name yet, but we will. We don't know where you are yet, but we will. The one thing that we do know right now is *what* you are. You are a worthless coward and a bully. You hide behind Allah's word, you kill in God's name, but that doesn't disguise your true character. You are a pathetic and spineless murderer."

Jefferson Blake paused again, scanning the room like a lion waiting to be challenged, his features masked in concentration. When he resumed, it was directly into the television camera at the rear of the space. America may hear his words, but he spoke to only one person.

"And it is me you should come after, not the people who surround me. It was me who shot and killed your brother. It was my finger that pulled the trigger. This is now personal, it's between the two of us, no one else. But, I warn you, be wary. I carry with me the unbridled resolve that will end this story with me standing over your grave, arm in arm with my fellow apostles of freedom. As many before me, I have sought and found a depth of conviction that will see you and your kind of morally bankrupt killers stripped of your ability to threaten, bully and slaughter others… forever.

"Deeper than your hatred resides in you, my own resolve for the pursuit of freedom is boundless.

"I say to you, you better come after me soon, because if you don't, I am most certainly coming after you!"

A deafening applause ruptured the silence.

President Jefferson Blake left the podium and strode right past Greatrex and I standing in the corridor. We joined Abe Peterson in trying to keep up with his boss.

"What did you think, Abe?" asked the president.

"Sir, with respect, I thought it was both the most inspiring and the dumbest presidential speech I've ever heard."

The president smiled and walked on.

Chapter 28

Washington was never my favorite place in the world. Too much hustling and too many self-obsessed wannabes attempting to climb the political food chain. As we drove down Wisconsin Avenue toward the 495, I wondered what chance we'd have of tracking down Sua'd Bahri in this maze of humanity. Our intelligence had told us that the US capital was her intended destination, but so far neither the FBI nor the Secret Service had found any trace of her.

"What are the chances of success?" asked Greatrex, sitting next to me in the hire car. "Jumaa is in regular contact with the families and has his local Sudanese network running overtime, yet no one has heard anything."

"There's always the possibility that Bahri isn't even in Washington. When we interrupted their plans in Sudan, they probably took her to ground while they regrouped. She could be anywhere in the county," I added.

"The FBI will cast its net wide, but that's a lot of ground to cover."

"Too much," I said. "Plus, we're working against the clock here. It was a hell of a speech that the president made today, but he virtually called Atha Riek's brother out. 'Come and get me.'"

"I was wondering about that," Greatrex responded. "I'm sure he did it on purpose."

"The more we learn about Jefferson Blake, the more I reckon he does nothing by accident. His convictions drive him."

"I wish that happened more around this town."

"Amen to that," I replied.

"The question is, though, why *did* Blake do that? Why call him out? He basically urged him to attempt something soon."

"Try this," I suggested. "The president doesn't want this situation plaguing the country for too long. He's saying, 'Let's sort it now.' With the state visit coming up, he's setting the stage rather than letting Riek's brother take control."

"It also means that the terrorists may rush. He wouldn't have a vast amount of time to reformulate a bulletproof plan," said the big fella.

"Exactly," I replied. "Blake is laying down the rules."

"Cunning."

"Somehow I doubt Abe Peterson and his team are expressing that sentiment at the moment."

As we passed through the enormous stone gates of the general's estate in Maryland and headed up the winding drive, I felt the events of the day catch up with me. What we needed was a drink and some downtime. General Devlin-Waters had offered to put us up while we were in Washington; he had plenty of room in his sprawling mansion. As I considered the evening ahead, I was sure we would get the drink, but maybe not the downtime.

There were other complications. I would be sleeping under the same roof as Kaitlin Reed. Nicholas Sharp: the man who brings it all upon himself.

189

"So," began the general," ensconced in his favorite winged armchair in the mansion's formal lounge room, "we have a lot to talk about."

"Yes sir, we do," I agreed. I hoped he was talking about the terrorists and not Kaitlin.

He was.

"First things first. While everyone is searching for Sua'd Bahri, I suggest we focus on the state visit. That seems like the most feasible time that an attack would happen if Atha Riek's brother wants to take out both presidents."

"Agreed," said Greatrex, "but my gut is telling me that the state dinner is also the most likely event within the visit."

"Why so? asked the general.

"A couple of reasons," replied Greatrex. "Number one, I reckon an assassination at the state dinner would make more of a public statement, and public statements are what terrorists are all about."

"And number two," I chipped in, "Jefferson Blake did almost everything except send Riek's brother an invitation to the dinner."

"Yes," replied the general. "I agree. It may have been a very smart move by the president, naming the time and place."

"Maybe yes, maybe no," observed Jumaa, who was once again with us. "Riek's brother will be many things, most of them bad, but he is not a fool. You cannot survive hidden in plain sight for over thirty years without being very shrewd. Besides, his planning skills must be outstanding. The Shararaa have been consistently effective despite their limited numbers. As you Americans say, they punch well above their weight."

"Thanks for making us feel that much better, my friend," I responded, tongue firmly in cheek. "But I sense you're right.

We are dealing with a mind who thinks well ahead of the game."

"I believe you are all underestimating yourselves and the country's security services," announced Kaitlin Reed as she walked into the room.

I sat up straight in my armchair. Boyish charm.

"Each one of you is right," declared the general. He got up and moved in front of the fireplace as Kaitlin flopped down. "This terrorist is smart, we are smart, the security services are smart. It comes down to who predicts the other's behavior first."

"And who will risk everything to be the last one standing at the end," I added.

"Precisely," said our former leader. "That is why I'm putting my money on the people in this room."

No pressure there.

Two hours later we'd all agreed that outside the immediate search for Salah's wife, planning a strategy for the state dinner was our highest priority. Ideas bounced around like popping corn, until finally, we had a plan.

"Well, that's it," declared the general. "To sum up our thoughts: Nicholas is P.D. Bailey's keyboardist, meaning that both he and Jack will be at the dinner. I'll arrange for the White House to appoint Kaitlin as assistant events manager for the banquet. She can help the president's daughter, Cassandra, plan the affair. Given Kaitlin's tour-managing background, that shouldn't be a problem. Jumaa, through your role as the president's special advisor on Sudan, you'll volunteer to be the liaison coordinator with the Sudanese government's team."

"These arrangements should, between us, offer a broad

landscape of the whole event, both in its planning and on the night."

"It sounds like a thorough plan when you put it that way," said Greatrex.

"Yes, particularly when you consider that this is all on top of the president's regular security," noted Kaitlin.

I looked across the space at Jumaa. He understood the reach of the Shararaa better than any of us. Shoulders hunched forward, he tapped repeatedly on the arm of his chair.

"It's good," I said, "but is it good enough?" Nicholas Sharp: glass half-empty.

Everyone in the room was silent. No one seemed to want to answer my question.

Finally, Jumaa spoke up. "No, it is not good enough. Everything we've planned, the Shararaa will expect. If they keep coming at the president, either president, it is because they know how to deal with the measures that are in place."

"Then what do you suggest?" asked the general.

Stone-cold silence.

I leaned back in my chair, took a deep breath and waited a moment before speaking. Then I told them all what I had in mind.

Chapter 29

Ten days had gone by with no news on Sua'd Bahri's location. The authorities had swept the city and come up dry. Jumaa's network of Sudanese residents had fared no better. With only another ten days until the state visit, we had no fresh intelligence to help us.

Like everyone else, Greatrex and I felt frustrated beyond words. We couldn't act if we had no information to act on. My phone rang as we ate a leisurely breakfast in the general's kitchen.

"Nicholas, it's Abe Peterson."

"What's up?"

"We might have a breakthrough, even if only a small one. A local resident down here in Gaithersburg, Montgomery County, says she saw a woman matching Bahri's description being led into an apartment complex on Frederick Avenue. She couldn't make a positive ID from the photo but said it may well be our girl."

"Have you been down there?" I asked.

"We're here now, with our FBI colleagues, about to go in."

"Jack and I are on our way. Text me the address."

"Will do, but you better hurry. If the press gets hold of this, they'll be all over it in no time. If you and Jack want to stay off the radar, you don't want to be seen here."

"Got it."

Thirty minutes later, Greatrex and I pulled up outside an aging apartment building set well back off Frederick Avenue. The cinder-block construction and the 'old but not yet retro' architecture told us that this wasn't an upmarket complex. The age and condition of the cars out the front confirmed the impression.

We got out of the car. I called Abe. "We're here."

"Come on up. Apartment 317 on the top floor. Although there's not much point, it's a bust."

A young female agent who seemed not long out of Quantico let us in the front door. Abe Peterson stood in the apartment's cramped lounge room talking with a tall man in an FBI raid jacket.

"Nicholas, Jack, this is Special Agent Doug Humphries."

We shook hands.

"I'm afraid there's nothing here to see," said Humphries.

Abe nodded in agreement. "Whoever was here has bolted. We can't even confirm if it was our girl."

"We have agents going door to door," added Humphries.

"I've pulled my people off," added Abe. "If they start flashing Secret Service credentials, someone will call the press."

"Do you mind if we poke around?" I asked.

Humphries looked at Peterson, who nodded.

"Sure thing," he answered, "but touch nothing."

"Got it," I replied.

It didn't take Greatrex and I long to explore the apartment. Two small bedrooms, a kitchenette attached to the lounge and a tiny bathroom. The entire place appeared somewhere between clean and dirty, non-committed.

I walked into the bathroom. Signs of recent habitation were obvious: cosmetics, toothpaste, and some over-the-counter medications in the cabinet.

"Whoever left here didn't take a long time to pack," said Greatrex.

"Or they didn't need this stuff where they were going," I replied.

One step to my right and I looked down at a bin. A few cellophane wrappers that would have come from the medications lay at the bottom. I was just turning away when a plastic jar under the wrappers caught my eye. I kneeled down for a closer inspection. There was no label, but there was one pill in the bottom of the jar. I poured the pill into my palm and read the number stamped on it: *IP 110.*

"That's Vicodin," said Special Agent Humphries as he entered the compact room. "We'll bag it and send it to the lab, but I doubt they'll come up with much."

"Vicodin's a painkiller," I responded. Nicholas Sharp: insightful observer.

"It is," replied Humphries, "but that means little. Someone here may have been in some pain, equally they may have been dealing in opioids. I'm sure you're aware there's an opioid crisis in our country at the moment. They wouldn't be the first dealer in this neighborhood."

"You're right," I said. "It could mean anything... or nothing."

I brushed passed the agent and went back to join Greatrex and Abe Peterson in the lounge room. As Humphries left the bathroom, he tripped on a piece of torn linoleum. His hand automatically reached out to the door handle for support.

"Damn, they haven't fingerprinted that doorknob yet," he exclaimed. "I suppose it doesn't matter for shit anyway, there are plenty more."

As he lifted his fingers off the door handle, he swore again. "Double shit, there's something sticky on the doorknob." The agent raised his hand to his face and looked at the yellow sap like substance stuck to his palm. "Well, that just about confirms it," he said.

"Confirms what?" asked Abe Peterson.

"I'd bet my pension that this stuff is cannabis resin, or more accurately cannabis rosin."

"Rosin, what do you mean?" I inquired.

"Rosin is the new thing," replied Humphries. "They take almost any cannabis product like a flower or hash and add high heat and pressure. The process produces solventless hash oil. It's a quick, and not too difficult, method that yields a golden sap with extremely high potency."

"Well, you learn something new every day," said Greatrex.

"Yup," replied Humphries. "And that means they used this place as some sort of drug-processing facility."

"It's more than likely that the woman our witness observed coming in here merely needed to feed her habit," added Abe.

"Right," agreed the FBI agent, "but we'll get the pill bottle tested, anyway."

Peterson turned to Greatrex and I. "Sorry guys, we've wasted your time coming down here."

"Not to worry," I replied. "We had nothing better to do."

We shook hands and the big fella and I left the building.

Just as we climbed into our car in front of the apartment block, I heard a voice.

"Mr. Sharp, Mr. Sharp, could I have a word with you?"

I looked up to see Joe Connors, the journalist who'd introduced himself as a freelancer working for *Time* at Jefferson Blake's press conference. *Damn.*

I saw little point in denying who I was, but I could certainly feign not knowing him.

"Yes, I'm Nicholas Sharp, but I'm sorry, do I know you?"

"My name is Joe Connors, sir. I'm a freelance journo currently employed by *Time* magazine."

"Yes, Mr. Connors. What can a humble musician such as myself do for you?"

"I think we both know that you are a little more than just a humble musician, Mr. Sharp. Please take a look at this."

The journalist drew a cell phone out of his pocket. Set on the gallery app, it featured a single photograph. A crouching figure cast in a dim light appeared: me. It was a long-distance shot taken with a telephoto lens. I was certain of that because no one would have been up close at that moment. If they had, I would've shot them. My hand held a gun, and almost out of the image, but still clearly visible, was the face of Jefferson Blake.

The night of our escape from the Shararaa camp.

"Is there anything you would like to tell me, Mr. Sharp?"

Greatrex had moved around the car and was now standing behind me. "Is there a problem?"

I showed him the phone. He grunted.

"No, Mr…. er… Connors, I've nothing to say to you." This wasn't the first time a photo had got me into trouble.

"It would be better if we talked, Mr. Sharp. You may know I've recently returned from Sudan, where I researched President Blake's extradition from the county."

"Yes, I think I saw your face on television, at that press conference."

"Now, Mr. Sharp, please don't go playing games with me. I've been around a bit too long for that."

"What do you want me to say, Mr. Connors?"

"I want the full story of Jefferson Blake's escape from Sudan from beginning to end… exclusively."

I felt frozen in the moment. A well-thought response seemed as scarce as the hair on Jack Greatrex's head.

"And if I choose not to talk to you, Mr. Connors?"

"If you don't talk, I will publish everything I have, including your name. Presuming that Mr. Greatrex here was the man with you in Sudan, I will, of course, publish his name too."

Greatrex grunted again.

I thought for a moment.

"I'm afraid I can't help you, Mr. Connors. All you have is one photograph that some overimaginative person has Photoshopped together to make up a fascinating bit of fiction."

There's a reason I don't play poker.

Connors smiled. Smug. "I'm sorry, Mr. Sharp, I also possess video of an interview recorded with an eyewitness to your escapades. One of the Shararaa guards up on the surrounding hills that night."

This wasn't getting any better.

"As previously stated, I've nothing to say to you. Now, if you excuse us, we need to go."

Connors shrugged his shoulders. For a moment, I thought he would back off. I was wrong.

"Mr. Sharp, I understand your surprise. You'll require a little time to process this. I'll give you my number. Please call me by the end of the evening."

He produced a business card.

"Oh, one more thing. As a gesture of goodwill, to let

198

you know I am a man of scruples, I'll share some additional information that may benefit you."

Neither Greatrex nor I responded. We just stood like fools, staring vacantly at the journalist.

"My informant tells me the Shararaa have added three more names to their hit list. These people seem very upset with you."

With that, Joe Connors turned and walked away.

Chapter 30

Greatrex and I drove into Georgetown. The busy area was littered with throngs of people and a score of eateries. We needed to sit and talk. Joe Connors's news had muted our appetites, but not our thirst. We chose an out-of-the-way Mexican café, sat down at a table at the rear, and ordered two beers with a plate of nachos. The food remained untouched by the time we hit our second beer.

"So, if we let this Connors guy publish, we will cop a tsunami of life-changing publicity, all of it uncomfortable," said the big fella.

"I agree."

"I can't think of too much worse," he continued.

"It would also mean we couldn't attend the state dinner. The critics would say that having someone else on the Shararaa's assassination list at the dinner would be reckless. We'd be out of the picture."

"Okay, thanks," said Greatrex, "you thought of something worse."

"You know I'm loath to be in the spotlight here. Despite being in the music industry, it's just not our style. Would we be smarter walking away from the whole situation?"

"Explain."

"Well, the Secret Service protects Jefferson Blake. These people have kept presidents alive for decades if not hundreds of years."

"Mostly."

"Yeah, all right, point taken," I replied. "What good are we doing here? We're just a couple of amateurs. Take this morning's little investigation in Gaithersburg. I'm busy looking for reds under the beds while the FBI professionals put the actual picture together in five minutes. As detectives, we're out of our league."

"So, we walk away," said Greatrex. "The trouble with that is that we'd still cop the publicity. Although you'd do well on the talk-show circuit, don't forget we'd also have a death sentence looming over our heads from our friends the Shararaa."

"You make a fair point."

"Besides…"

"When did we ever walk away from anything just because we were out of our depth?"

"My case rests," said Greatrex.

We sat sipping our beers. An idea formed in my mind, a way out. It must have been the alcohol.

"What if…" I began. "What if we spoke to Abe Peterson and did a deal? Give Connors the full story… under certain conditions?"

"What conditions?"

"He only publishes after the state dinner, and he leaves ours and Jumaa's names out of it. We'll then give him the entire thing from our arrival in Sudan to the very end. He can write a damn book if he wants."

Greatrex paused. "It's worth a try."

Our hunger reappeared, and we tore into our lunch.

Georgetown was bustling, late lunches turning into evening drinks. Small groups of the Washington ambitious, coming and going. Did anyone ever do any work around here? It was midafternoon by the time we left the crowds and returned to our car. We had parked it well off the main drag down a small laneway just off Potomac Street.

I was considering our plan. We'd have a chance. It would mean we would have to get White House approval. I'd be spending the afternoon on the phone...

"Nicholas."

"Jack, I reckon..." I looked up as I spoke. I wished I hadn't.

There were six of them. They were huge, of African descent, possibly Sudanese. More pointedly, they were armed. I saw no Kalashnikovs, but they didn't need more than the handguns they were aiming at us. I mentally kicked myself for our lack of caution.

"The Riek family sends their regards," said the man closest to me. As he smiled his broken and uneven teeth lent an evil menace to his grin. I held no doubt he was a fighter.

"You won't get away with kidnapping us here in broad daylight," replied Greatrex, standing his ground.

From where I was standing, it looked like they would. They'd parked a large black van with blocked out windows two spaces in front of ours. Its rear doors were open.

"Who said anything about kidnapping?" declared the fighter, his Sudanese accent unmistakable. "The street crime in Washington is terrible. Two more victims won't crack a headline."

For a brief moment, I considered other times I'd faced down an enemy, both in the Marines and since. I'd always found a way out. It was my sniper's training, kicking in with a plan, even if it was impromptu.

But there was no plan in sight.

Each man was at least two yards from Greatrex and I, too great a distance to bridge without being shot. If we each took out one man, that would leave four more.

Still no plan.

Greatrex's agitation began to show. He kicked the ground, fists balled and forearms tensed. I knew what followed that. He would go down fighting. While I respected his intention, he'd still end up going down. We both would.

"All right," I said, putting my mouth into gear, having no idea what words were about to come out. "How about a deal?"

No response.

I continued. "I understand you people want us dead—can't blame you—but what if we could offer you the bigger prize? We are close to President Blake. We can give him to you."

Greatrex stopped his work-up. He knew I was lying through my teeth, but we needed our assailants to think otherwise.

"Nicholas, don't be stupid," he said. "I get you hate politicians, but he's the president."

"Shut up, Jack," I hissed.

"Nice little show," observed the fighter, "but why would you help us when you know we'd kill you later, anyway?"

"Show some backbone, Nicholas," said Greatrex.

The two men closest to the big fella appeared nervous. They repeatedly changed their weight from foot to foot. I needed to distract them before they pulled their triggers.

"Blake has done nothing for us. We risked our lives to get him out of Sudan for naught. Reluctant heroes who fade back into obscurity is his plan. You heard his press conference. That left us with nothing, and we're pissed."

For a split second, I saw hesitation on the fighter's face. I pressed my case.

"If you've been following us today, you would have noted that we met with a journalist. Joe Connors, he was the one who blew this entire Sudan thing wide open. You'd have seen him on the news."

No reaction, but no bullets.

"We met to tell him we'd provide the full story, every goddamn part of it. We'll let the world understand who the heroes are here. That self-obsessed, condescending dickhead Blake can go to hell."

The fighter put up a palm, calming his men.

"If we allow you to help us, what are you offering?" he asked.

"We can get you into the dinner," I said.

"We are already in," replied one of the other men.

I glanced at Greatrex.

"If your plan fails, you will have two more people to aid you. Surely you can't get that many bodies into the White House?" I paused. "Or better still hold my friend here with you. That way you have guaranteed my help." I hoped that would stop them shooting Greatrex on the spot.

The fighter seemed to hesitate. "There may be merit in what you say, although you would only delay your own deaths. Our leader, however, does not enjoy deviating from plans. I must make a call."

"You better make it quick," I said. "Any minute now a police patrol might pass here, and all bets will be off."

The fighter hesitated, just for a second. "Grab them and put them in the van."

That was all we needed.

The two men closest to Greatrex came up to him, clasping

an arm each. They'd put their guns away so they could use two hands. The two men closest to me did the same. We didn't resist, we wanted them relaxed.

The fighter led the way toward the van as the last man, still armed, brought up the rear.

As we reached the vehicle, Greatrex and I each lunged toward a captor. I didn't have time to look after that. I shoved the man on my right, slipped my hand inside his jacket and wheeled him sideways, placing him between me and the guard whose grasp I'd shaken free. I figured I had less than two seconds to make this work. My fingers wrapped around the icy steel grip of his gun as I squeezed the trigger, the weapon still in its holster. It was a risk to assume that the safety was still off. It was.

The man grunted in pain but didn't go down. The other guard was now coming around him to get at me. In two quick movements, I elbowed the approaching guard in the face and pulled the gun out of the first man's holster. The second guard reached under his jacket, and I fired a round into his chest before he could get to his weapon. My original guard then slugged me hard in the side of the face. I felt dazed but held the man tight.

Another three gunshots. The man I held collapsed in my arms. I looked up to see the rear guard had fired in my direction but hit his colleague by mistake. Before I could raise my gun toward him, a red stain appeared on his chest. Greatrex had shot him.

I whirled around toward the fighter. He'd leaped behind one of the open van doors and was now taking aim at Greatrex, his gun arm protruding around the door. Raising my weapon, I fired through the blacked-out window where I figured his head would be. As the glass shattered, he fell to the ground.

Greatrex. I turned just as the big fella put a shot through the head of the man whose gun he had taken.

Twenty seconds and it was over.

I looked over at Greatrex. "Show some backbone, you say."

Chapter 31

We were again sitting around the general's lavish lounge room. I was on my third Scotch and reliving the day for the benefit of Kaitlin, Jumaa and the general himself.

"So, the FBI took over the scene of the shooting in no time at all. Along with Homeland Security, they immediately labeled it as a terrorist act and brought down a media blackout on the entire affair."

"What about the journalist... Connors?" asked Kaitlin.

"Abe Peterson spoke to the president on our behalf. Blake was fine with our proposed deal, so I called Joe Connors half an hour ago to confirm it," I replied.

"Will this man honor the arrangement?" inquired Jumaa.

"A fair question and we can't know the answer with absolute certainty. He says he will, and he's reputed to be a straight shooter," I responded.

"Speaking of being a straight shooter, you two are very lucky to have made it out of that alleyway alive today," said Kaitlin.

A slight quiver laced her voice, exposing her concern. I just wasn't sure how deep the disquiet ran, or, in fact, how deep I wanted it to run.

"Yes, we were fortunate," chipped in Greatrex. "Who thought Nicholas could be such a convincing sniveling rat?"

"Thank you... I think."

"What we need to focus on here is that brief conversation between you two and the Shararaa assassins." The general, straight to the point as ever. "Nicholas, you mentioned that you offered to get them into the state dinner."

"Yes, sir, I did. They said they were already in."

"That is concerning," replied the general. "These terrorists must be sure of their plan if they didn't jump at your proposition."

"It's a worry," I responded.

"And nothing came of your visit to the apartment in Montgomery County?" asked Kaitlin.

"No, it was a false alarm," said Greatrex. "It had nothing to do with our search for Sua'd Bahri, although the FBI is running some tests on some materials found there.

"So, we're back to square one," declared the general.

"Not square one," I replied. "We're now certain the Shararaa are feeling confident in their plan to assassinate both the presidents. We can also assume from their response to my offer it is more than likely the state dinner will be the event they target."

"Don't forget we know that Jumaa, you, and I have been added to the Shararaa's list of people to kill," added the big fella.

"Thanks for the reminder, but there is one other thing. The Shararaa are now down six of their men because of this afternoon's efforts." I almost sounded proud.

Jumaa got up from his chair and shuffled over to join the general at the fireplace. Once again, he showed signs of discomfort; shoulders tensed, brow crinkled.

"Nicholas, with all due respect to the resourcefulness that

you and Jack displayed this afternoon, I would warn you, never, ever, underestimate the ability of the Shararaa to surprise you," he declared.

So much for pride.

"You will need to be careful in your movements," instructed the general.

"I don't think they'll try to take us out again before the state dinner, in case we disrupt their plans further," I said. "But after the dinner, everything changes."

"I will talk some sense into Jefferson Blake and his people," announced the general. "He should cancel this damn dinner until we can sort this out."

"With due respect, sir, I disagree," I replied.

The general looked surprised at my comment. He wasn't used to being disagreed with.

I continued. "President Blake knows exactly what he's doing. He's bringing the game onto his turf and with his timing. If we can't put an end to this plot now, he, the country, and, for that matter, Jack, Jumaa, and I, will all be under threat from these bastards from here until eternity."

"Hmph," responded the general.

The room then faded to an uneasy silence.

"Are you saying, Nicholas, that in the meantime, there is nothing we can do?" asked Kaitlin.

There was no painless way to put it. "We have no choice. It's game on."

Chapter 32

But it wasn't a game.

Abe Peterson ushered me through the doors at the White House visitors' entrance on East Executive Avenue. The black rings under his eyes spoke of too much lost sleep.

"I'm convinced this is the worst idea in the history of presidential protection," he said.

I shook his hand, but I couldn't allay his fears.

"I'm sorry, Abe, the weight of the democratic world seems to be sitting on your shoulders."

The special agent led me across the vast East Wing lobby. We passed several security personnel. Each one stood down with a nod from Abe. We were walking through the garden room before he spoke again.

"I've tried everything I can to persuade the president to cancel this event tonight, but he won't budge."

"You're not alone there. General Devlin-Waters attempted the same approach. He told me that Jefferson Blake wouldn't even entertain the idea," I replied.

"I can't help but respect the man for his courage, the same goes with the Sudanese president, but it doesn't make my job any easier."

I nodded.

We walked along the east colonnade. The area was closed in, but through the windows the view across the White House gardens, was spectacular.

"This part of the complex is usually accessible to the public when viewing the building. We've canceled all tours for the last week. There are a lot of unhappy tourists out there."

"The price you pay," I said.

We entered the main White House structure through another large foyer. Once again, the gravitas of the situation hit me. We were in one of the most famous buildings on the planet, and we were here to protect the leader of the free world. I felt my shoulders slump at the thought. I could only imagine the burden playing on the mind of the Secret Service agent beside me.

Abe Peterson led me down a wide center hall at a cracking pace. I had to work hard to keep up. Glancing to my left, I looked through a doorway to see the famed China Room. They had made history in this building for centuries; I worried about the history that may be made in the next twelve hours.

Peterson pushed through another doorway, this one leading to the famous western colonnade, the president's route to work in the Oval Office each day. As we walked past the Rose Garden, it was a hive of activity. This is where the state dinner would take place, and where I would perform with P.D. Bailey and his band later in the evening.

"Most state dinners are held in the State Dining Room," announced the agent. "Although there is precedence, our security hasn't been helped by this event being held outdoors."

Ten minutes afterward, we were sitting in a sizable room scattered with desks, massive screens and a crowd of agents.

"Welcome to our command center," Peterson said, waving

an arm across the space. "This is where we monitor everything that happens in the White House complex. Tonight, this place will be our 'eyes on.'"

It was impressive. I was sitting in the company of some of the world's best security operators.

"Jack Greatrex is up at the stage area completing your equipment set up, Nicholas. I wanted to take this opportunity to talk things through with you."

I nodded.

"This is a more than unusual situation. Civilians rarely find themselves here. In your case, President Blake insisted, and I agreed, that you be in on our detail's communication loop this evening. I think we all understand that you and Jack have more than proved your loyalty to POTUS." The agent paused. "I would add, however, that if the shit hits the fan, don't get in our way."

Again, I just nodded.

"Without going into all the specifics, know that every available special agent and special officer in the protective detail will be here tonight. Personal leave and less important assignments are playing second fiddle to tonight's dinner. We've also tripled the uniformed officers on duty."

Many people think the uniformed security personnel that protect the White House are Marines. In fact, they're members of the Secret Service Uniformed Division.

"Nicholas, our Investigative Division, along with all the other investigating agencies involved have come up with no fresh information. We cannot locate Atha Riek's brother."

"It's hard to imagine how someone embedded in such a dangerous organization could stay off the radar so long, but somehow he's done it," I responded.

"And, to be honest, that scares the hell out of me," said Peterson.

The special agent paused again. He looked like he was searching for the right words.

"It's because of this monster's ability to disappear that I agreed to you and Jack Greatrex being part of our security here tonight, Nicholas."

That was perplexing.

"The Secret Service can protect, and we can investigate. We do both damn well. The trouble is, we do not understand who we are protecting the president from. I'm aware you haven't laid eyes on the brother, but you have seen Riek up close."

I saw where this was going.

"They are twins, if not identical. Should you see any man who bears even the slightest resemblance to Atha Riek in any way—eyes, chin, mannerisms—I want you to inform us immediately. I don't care how many security credentials they hold, I want to know."

"Fair enough," I said, "but what about Sua'd Bahri?"

Abe Peterson shrugged his shoulders, briefly casting his eyes down.

"That one has us beat. We're confident she was bound for Washington—you figured that out. We can only assume that she is part of the Shararaa's plan to assassinate the president, but apart from that, we've got nothing. To be honest, we don't even have a working theory as to what her role is. She may be the blunt weapon, she may function as a support person, or she may be dead."

Peterson sat back in his chair.

"Abe, I've no answer for you there. If I did, you would already know, but I've got to tell you, in my gut I'm certain she's part

213

of the plan," I said.

"And it's because of that we've set up the system you requested," replied the special agent.

"Let me talk you through it."

Chapter 33

The lights across the Rose Garden glimmered like fireflies dancing in the darkness. An array of designer table settings covered the length and breadth of the space. The Sudanese national colors—red, white, black, and green—dominated. While most of the tables were round, there was a longer, rectangular table at the southern end. This was for the A-team; the president's party, including his guest of honor. To the right of that was a small stage with a podium featuring an eagle's crest; that's where the speeches would happen.

The VIP guests would arrive soon. White House staff, entertainers, and caterers scurried about under the watchful eye of the Secret Service. Agents dressed in black suits hovered everywhere, with many more stationed across the whole complex. Tactical teams on standby remained hidden in undisclosed parts of the grounds.

"It's quite something, isn't it?" said Greatrex, who had materialized beside me.

"Sure is," I responded. "When the president of the United States of America throws a party, it's certain to be a hell of a show."

Greatrex nodded.

"Have you got the final running order?" I asked.

"Yup. After the initial pomp and ceremony of the presidential entrance, the president will receive his guests in the Blue Room. After that, once everyone has moved out here, the culinary part of the event begins while the United States Marine Band plays a selection of dinner music."

As Greatrex spoke, he waved his hand toward the buildings on the north and west sides of the garden. They'd set microphones up for the musicians under the porticos on both sides. Ordered in single rows, each musician would be bathed in individual light. It made for a very dynamic look. Members of the band were just starting to take their places. On the roof of the west portico, the rest of the band, lit by floodlights, would overlook the diners.

"After the main course," continued Greatrex, "a small Sudanese group, comprising both Western and traditional African instruments, will perform."

"That worried me when I was first told about it," I said, "but Abe Peterson assures me the musicians have been vetted and there is no security risk with any of them."

"I say we still keep a close eye on them," replied the big fella.

"Absolutely."

Greatrex continued with the rundown. "After the Sudanese band's performance, it's time for the speeches. Both presidents will have their moment in the spotlight as the Sudanese president presents a traditional Sudanese lyre to Jefferson Blake."

"I'm told that they've checked out the instrument being presented in every possible way. The strings have even been secured so no one can remove them to use as a garrote," I said.

"They're certainly taking no chances."

"No, we are dealing with the highest standard of professionalism—Abe Peterson and his men know their stuff." I hoped I sounded confident.

"Anyway," continued Greatrex, "straight after the presentation and the speeches, they'll serve dessert and you guys hit the stage. I'm thinking that's when the evening may loosen up a bit."

It would be very difficult to listen to P.D. Bailey perform his iconic brand of soul and blues without relaxing into the infectiousness of his music.

"So," I said, "when is the situation the most vulnerable? If the Shararaa intend to strike tonight, when will it be?"

The question was rhetorical. Despite all the professionals that had prepared for this event, nobody had a single clue.

Chapter 34

"The president is upstairs in the Yellow Oval Room entertaining the Sudanese leader and some high-ranking officials from both governments," announced Abe Peterson, appearing behind us. "I'm heading straight up there now, and I won't be leaving the president's side until the evening is over."

I glanced at Peterson. He looked as alert as a fox, but he couldn't hide the creases around his eyes that gave away his tiredness. Jefferson Blake's principles had taken their toll on this man.

"Have you seen anything that seems out of place?" he asked.

"Nothing," I responded. "All the musicians are doing musician-type things, no one stands out. All the other staff seem focused on their immediate tasks. I've noticed nobody casing the place."

"My men said the same thing. They're all aware you two are here and why. You've got a free pass to roam around as much as you like. Just let us know…"

"We'll tell you if we see anything out of the ordinary." Greatrex finished the agent's sentence for him.

The two of us wandered through the area. As we reached the northern end of the space, there was a bit of commotion. The musicians from the Sudanese group had arrived, now heading toward the stage to tune their instruments. They'd been told to leave them after their sound check in the afternoon. Musicians don't enjoy being too far from their instruments; to them, they are like family and should be kept close.

Greatrex and I inspected each band member as they passed us. There was nothing familiar about any of them. While I held total faith in the White House vetting process, I held more faith in our own judgment. In preparation, Jack and I went over pictures of every known Shararaa associate and every possible acquaintance of Atha Riek. All we saw in the band were warm, smiling faces.

It was time to test my back-up plan. Fixed to a button on each of Greatrex and my jackets was a small camera. The cameras linked directly to a room in the adjacent treasury building where Salah Bahri was monitoring a screen. Two experienced Secret Service agents and an FBI operative accompanied him. We were all in the same communication loop. My thinking was that there was a possibility that Salah may note some movement, some bit of body language that would give Sua'd away if she had disguised her appearance and been able to make it this far. No one can read a person's body language like their spouse. The idea was far-fetched, but Abe Peterson agreed to it. When you are all out of ideas, anything is worth trying.

"Can you hear me, Salah?" I asked.

"Sure, Mr. Sharp," came Salah's voice into my earbud.

"We just passed the musicians; did you spot anything?"

"No, sir, nothing familiar. I know I would have recognized Sua'd no matter how she altered her look."

I reckoned the same, yet it was disappointing. Salah told us that Sua'd played the violin when she was at school. I thought we may have had a break there, but clearly not.

"We'll check out all the Sudanese guests and government officials the same way, as we come across them," I said. "Stay alert."

In the distance, the strains of 'Hail to the Chief' emanated from the White House itself. President Blake and his daughter Cassandra were about to make their entrance. I caught Greatrex's attention, and we wandered over.

They say the British do pageantry better than anybody, but the sight of Jefferson Blake and his daughter accompanied by the Sudanese president and his spouse, descending the stairs to the resounding applause of their elegantly dressed guests put the Brits on notice.

There was applause at their entrance and more applause when the band played the Sudanese national anthem. The two presidents then formally greeted each guest as they lined up: American hospitality at the highest level.

Just as it had been that night in Khartoum several months earlier when the presidents last met at a social gathering, the room was a mass of color and vibrancy. Among the black dinner suits were the regal gowns of the Washington socialites combined with some stunning greens, reds and yellows worn by the Sudanese.

I'd studied the guest list carefully. It consisted of the politically important, the businessmen attempting to break into a fresh market, the pillars of the US Sudanese community and members of the visiting Sudanese entourage.

I supposed it looked odd as Greatrex and I moved around, working the room, attempting to get a shot of any relevant face we could find. I felt like a social misfit looking for a group to join, as I elbowed my way into several small gatherings while lining up an image for the camera.

"Anything at all?" I asked into the microphone clipped onto my sleeve.

"Nothing, sir," Salah responded.

I kept moving, watching, worrying. Across the garden, I saw Greatrex doing the same.

I found it impossible to reconcile that someone here planned to assassinate these two world leaders… well, *almost* impossible.

Chapter 35

An hour later, the Rose Garden was a hive of conversation. The Marine Band played, and the guests at the tables did whatever they came here to do, chatting, networking, social climbing, scoring political points.

At the head table, Jefferson Blake appeared relaxed and in control. He knew the stakes; he knew the dangers. The man was either naïve, or he had implicit trust in those protecting him; I would never have described this president as naïve.

For the thousandth time, I scanned the room, trying to take in each face as a separate entity, a separate threat. I had nothing.

Achieving little else, I went over to the entertainers' tent some distance away from the crowd. I needed to check in with P.D. and the band. My invitation to the event did say musician.

"Hey, Nicholas," called Brian Pitt, our drummer. "What about all this?" he asked, waving his arm toward the manicured lawn and the VIP diners. "Who would have thought?"

"I've played some dives, and I've played some big shows," added Barry Flannigan, our veteran bass player, "but I'll tell you, playing at the White House is something special." There wasn't much Barry hadn't done. In all the times we'd shared a stage, I'd never seen him flustered by anything. This moment seemed as 'in awe' as he got.

"Well hello, Nicholas, how's my favorite keys-man this evening?" There was no mistaking the raspy voice of the inimitable P.D. Bailey. "You look a little on edge," he added.

"Just inspired by the moment, P.D." I replied.

"Son, I've played here for four US presidents. It's always a big do."

Four presidents, impressive résumé.

"I'll tell you two things. Number one, I reckon this guy, Blake, is my favorite. He's the real thing," he continued.

I nodded in agreement. "And?"

"For all the times I've been here, I've never felt tension in the air like I'm sensing here tonight. You wouldn't know anything about that, would you?"

A very observant man was our P.D. Bailey.

"No, sir, I can't say I do."

I looked to the ground. Who would lie to an American icon?

I strolled back toward the guests, mainly to avoid having to deceive my musician friends any further. Jumaa sat at a table in the center of the garden. He excused himself and walked over to me.

"Anything?" he asked.

"That's the most popular question tonight," I replied, "but no news."

"I've been trying to mingle with as many of the Sudanese guests as I can," he continued. "Like everyone else, I've found no additional information. Although, it has been difficult to get close to the Sudanese president's party. They seem on edge and are being extremely protective."

"That's probably because they're as wary of the situation as we are."

"True, you are most likely right. There are some in his group I could not talk to at all. I wanted to eyeball everyone," he added with an anxiousness in his voice.

"Keep trying," I responded. No one within the loop was needlessly reassuring their colleagues tonight.

As I watched my Sudanese friend return to his table, I turned around to see a familiar figure a couple of yards away.

"It's Nicholas Sharp, isn't it?"

"Yes," I replied, taking a minute to place the face. Then the penny dropped. "Special Agent Humphries," I added, recognizing the FBI man from our failed raid in Gaithersburg.

Humphries nodded as we shook hands. Over his shoulder, I saw the Sudanese musicians stepping onto the stage. I wanted to be around when they performed, both for cultural and security reasons. Being stuck in conversation with an FBI agent wasn't in my plan.

"Abe Peterson asked me along, kind of as an outside view," the agent began. "From what he told me, that's somewhat like your role here tonight."

I nodded. "Pretty much right," I replied, still staring over his shoulder while trying to conceal my impatience.

"It's a funny thing," said Humphries, ignoring my body language. "We got back the test results from the raid on that drug den. It turns out that the bottle you found in the bin had contained Vicodin. Strangely, however, the cannabis rosin sample I took turned out not to be cannabis at all. It was just straight organic rosin."

I'd half turned away when Humphries words registered. I thought I may have misheard. "What did you say?"

224

"I said the cannabis rosin wasn't cannabis at all."

The band began to play. My brain ran overtime. Vicodin... painkillers... rosin? The most common use for organic rosin is to put on a violin or cello bow, or it would make no sound as it passed over the strings. Vicodin... painkillers... why? Then it hit me.

I knew exactly why.

Chapter 36

"Peterson, I've got something," I yelled into my microphone as I strode toward the stage.

"Position," came the terse reply.

"Main stage. I've got an idea, but no proof…"

"All available agents to the primary stage area, but be subtle, ladies and gents. We're working on a hunch. Don't make a scene unless we have to." Peterson's instructions energized his team into action.

"Salah, do you have an image?" I asked.

"Yes, standing by, Mr. Sharp, but I see nothing yet."

"Give me a moment."

By the time I got to the stage, eight Secret Service agents had gathered at each end. The band played their second piece, while the audience sat enthralled. Nobody would break etiquette to chat while guest musicians performed. That made our job more difficult.

"Salah, I'll step along the front of the stage, I won't have long to catch each musician before I need to move on. Focus on the string players."

"Got it, Mr. Sharp."

The Secret Service agents tried to appear as inconspicuous as possible, but their hands rested inside their jackets, weapons ready. It wouldn't do anyone's career any good to misread the situation, jump too soon, and create a needless panic.

Out of the corner of my eye, I noticed Abe Peterson had left his post behind the president's table and was headed toward the stage.

As I ambled across the small dance area, Greatrex appeared. I raised my palm to stop him. Salah needed to remain focused only on the image from my camera.

I blocked people's view, but there was no alternative. At least eight string players performed in the band. I stopped in front of each for as long as reasonable. It didn't help that six of the eight were female.

"Nothing, nothing, no…" Salah's tone betrayed no hint of recognition.

I got to the last musician. She played a violin.

"No, nothing."

I didn't think myself wrong, but it was sure starting to look that way. At the risk of making a complete fool of myself, I tried for another pass.

"Anything, Salah, search for any telltale."

"I will, Mr. Sharp, but I have nothing."

I was wrong, that was all there was to it.

"No… wait, go back one. No, it can't be, it's not her, but…"

"But what?" I asked, my voice cracking with urgency.

Suddenly, it was Salah's voice that sounded strained, his words rushed. "When Sua'd was a teenager, there was a car accident. She had whiplash; her neck muscles remained permanently damaged. When she played violin, she couldn't bend her head to the correct angle. She had to use a special extended chin rest to keep her collar straight. That last violinist, the one in the back row, had the same set-up, but it

227

wasn't Sua'd. I'm certain of that."

I moved back two steps and stood in front of the violinist. She glanced up at me, just for a second, before burying back down into her music.

"All right, Salah, think outside the square. Imagine if Sua'd had received some major surgery."

Vicodin—the most common painkiller used after surgery. After plastic surgery.

"No, wait, it's not possible. That is not my Sua'd, but they are her eyes."

That was all it took. Abe Peterson, who had been listening to every word, commanded, "I want an agent either side of that violinist now. As the song finishes escort her off the stage and into my office. If she struggles, subdue her. If that doesn't work, shoot her."

"No!" echoed the sound of Salah's voice. My earpiece went dead as they cut him off.

Two Secret Service men stepped up onto the stage.

"Put your instrument down and come with us," instructed the agent on her right.

For a moment, it looked certain the woman would offer up a fight. Her face contorted as she jumped to her feet.

"No, no... you can't."

She struggled wildly as an agent grabbed each arm, her violin and bow crashing to the stage.

"Leave me alone, you don't know what you've done."

The anger passed as quickly as it arrived. The woman's shoulders sagged, her legs went limp, the agents now holding her upright. They guided her off the platform, surrounded by a dozen more as their feet touched the ground.

Together, the huddle moved off toward the West Wing.

A panicked buzz spread through the audience. Some stood up, making ready to leave, others stared at the stage, transfixed.

I turned to the band leader. "Play on."

Let music calm the savage beast.

Chapter 37

"You have ten seconds to give me your name, your actual name, or your world is about to fall apart." Peterson was leading the interrogation.

The woman sat handcuffed in the chair. Her bottom lip quivered as a tear slipped down her cheek. She offered no response.

"Not speaking will *not* be to your advantage," the special agent continued.

Still nothing.

Abe Peterson had allowed me to be present for the questioning; I was in the family now.

"All right, let me help you out here. Your name is Sua'd Bahri. You're married to Salah Bahri and have a young daughter named Thiyiba."

The floodgates opened. The single tear turned into a torrent. Her hands shook as she released an anguished wail. "No, please no!"

We waited several minutes as the woman composed herself enough to speak.

When she began, her voice sounded little more than a whisper. "If you know all of that," she said, "then you know by arresting me you have sentenced my daughter and my husband to death."

Her distress flushed the room with emotion.

"Your daughter and your husband are safe," replied Peterson. "They're now in US protective custody, as are your fellow prisoners from Batn-El-Hajar. The Shararaa terrorist camp has been destroyed."

"I do not believe you. You are lying."

Abe Peterson glanced at me. As he nodded, I suddenly knew why I was in the room.

"Sua'd, I need to tell you a story," I began.

When I'd finished the woman in front of me looked wide-eyed.

"I will say nothing until you bring me my husband and daughter." She crossed her arms and sat back into her chair like a petulant child.

Peterson didn't respond. Then he walked out of the office.

Two minutes later, the agent returned. "Your husband will be here in ten minutes. Your daughter is off site. That will take longer."

I could see his strategy, give a little, take a little.

"Will that do?"

The woman breathed a lengthy sigh. She still shook, but less so.

"I'll speak when my husband is here."

The arms remained folded.

Ten long minutes later, the door opened. Two Secret Service agents walked into the already crowded space. Standing between them was Salah Bahri.

Salah ran to his wife, kneeling down beside her chair. He wrapped his arms around her shoulders, while staring up at

Abe through a stream of defiant tears.

Abe Peterson ignored him and got down to business.

"If you are to have any chance of seeing freedom again in your lifetime, you'll need to cooperate with us, and you will need to do it right now."

Sua'd nodded, her open expression showing all the signs of submission.

"I'll tell you what I can."

Peterson sat down opposite her. "First, how did you plan to kill President Blake?"

"No, no… that was not my intention, nor my instruction." Sua'd's agitation sparked again, her voice peaking in anger. I thought her denial sounded sincere, but I guess they all did.

"You expect us to believe you undertook face-altering plastic surgery and smuggled yourself into the White House to play some music?" Peterson sounded edgy, his tone aggressive.

"I speak the truth. I will tell."

Peterson grunted. "Tell."

"They have held me captive with no contact with the outside world since I left the terrorist camp in the Batn-El-Hajar Mountains. They told me if I didn't do everything they asked of me, they would kill Salah and Thiyiba."

"What did these people ask you to do?"

"At first, nothing. They brought me to Washington in a private plane. Immediately, they took me to a clinic where I was instructed to cooperate with the surgeons who would alter my face. I didn't want to, but I had no choice if I wanted to save my family."

"And afterward?"

"We traveled to an apartment somewhere on the edge of the city, so I could recover from the operation. They gave me painkillers."

"Vicodin?" I interjected.

"Yes," she replied. "I recovered quickly, and my scars healed well."

"How many people stayed with you?"

"Always the same three men—all Sudanese, all Shararaa."

"What happened next?"

"After two weeks, they brought a violin to the apartment. They also brought some music for me to practice. I didn't understand why."

"The music that you performed tonight?" I inquired.

"Yes, at first, I found it difficult. I had not played for a very long time. But it all came back to me."

"What else did they give you?" asked Peterson.

"Only a new bow and some rosin."

Peterson paused his questioning. These answers were not what he expected.

"Tell me about your instructions tonight? What did you have to do when you got to the White House?"

"That was the thing, I had no other instructions. I just had to come and play."

Abe Peterson's face became clouded with anger.

"We know they sent you here to assassinate United States President Jefferson Blake. You may or may not have been working under duress, but we know what you came here to do."

"No, no, I…"

"If you are not honest with us, you will never see your family again."

"No, again, no… you don't understand." Sua'd's eyes welled with tears.

"No…"

Just then my earbud rang out, "Nicholas, you're due on stage."

The president of the United States waits for no man.

Chapter 38

They'll live forever in my heart
Our brothers lost along the path
Ain't nothing gonna stop us
Claiming what we're owed
As we proudly march down freedom's road

The words to P.D. Bailey's classic song echoed around the garden. The audience listened, transfixed by the powerful sentiment of the old bluesman's vocals. President Jefferson Blake sat at his table. At one point, I thought I caught him wiping a tear from his eye. Next to him, the Sudanese president perched straight and attentive. His country had also paid a great price to live in democracy.

As I belted out the fierce Hammond organ solo the song demanded, I put every available inch of my being into the music. They asked us to play the tune just before the two presidents made their speeches. It was to be a moment. It *was* a moment.

I knew I should share in the relief of those around me, and the music should transcend any hesitation within me, but something just didn't sit right, and I couldn't put my finger on it.

When the song finished, the audience, including the two presidents, stood applauding. Even the Marine Band clapped from their rooftop stage.

It was over. I needed to move on.

Jefferson Blake made his way to the podium, chatting with President Sabbir as they strode side by side. The order of events had been rearranged in the shadow of the sudden departure of the Sudanese violinist. After the US President's speech, both the heads of state would move to the front of the band stage where President Sabbir would present Blake with the decorative lyre. The instrument lay on display on a stand at the corner of the platform. One of the Sudanese official party would retrieve it to pass to their president. After the presentation concluded, we were to continue playing. We'd been directed to remain on stage throughout the speeches.

"Ladies and gentlemen, the president of the United States," came the voice of the executive master of ceremonies.

Blake took to the podium as more applause resounded around the space. The man exuded confidence.

"Ladies and gentlemen, good evening and welcome…"

As much as I wanted to, I struggled to focus on the president's words. Fragments of information were hitting my brain like hail on a cracking windscreen. What had just happened here?

"Together we celebrate the foundation of liberty and free thought that our two nations strive for …"

Sua'd Bahri had seemed genuinely upset at the accusation that she was here to kill the president, surprised even. But maybe she'd been surprised because we caught her.

"Like our own battles, the road to freedom for our friends in

Sudan has not been easy. In fact, I know that from firsthand experience."

Nervous laughter from the crowd.

Sua'd and Salah's reactions seemed sincere when they saw each other. Their behavior didn't indicate a conspiracy.

"As P.D. Bailey just sang to us, 'They'll live forever in my heart, our brothers lost along the path.' Many honorable people, men and women, have fallen as both our great nations have fought for freedom. We will not forget them. Our gratitude is eternal."

If Sua'd was telling the truth, why in God's name was she here tonight? What possible benefit would the Shararaa gain from her being here?

"I say to you all, it is time to move forward, to celebrate who we are as nations, and what each of our glorious countries stand for on the world stage…"

Could Sua'd have been used to smuggle a weapon into the event, a bomb, perhaps? No, no chance. Security at the White House ran way too tight for that. Besides, the Secret Service agents had now removed her instrument, and its case. They took no chances.

Blake was winding up.

"So, in conclusion, I would like to thank President Sabbir and all our Sudanese friends who were unable make it here tonight. Welcome to the United States of America!"

The resounding applause filled the Rose Garden with warmth. Again, the guests rose to their feet.

Again, I had nothing.

Chapter 39

At the podium, Jefferson Blake stepped to one side, allowing President Sabbir to begin his address.

"Thank you so much for your warm welcome, Mr. President..."

I gazed across the garden. From the performer's stage, I had an unobstructed view of the guests. Two tables of high-level Sudanese sat with their US counterparts, paying dutiful attention to their leaders. Scanning the perimeters, I noticed nothing out of the ordinary apart from Jack Greatrex failing to blend in as he scrutinized the crowd from the northern portico. At the entrance to the garden area, I saw Kaitlin Reed also casting a watchful eye. Team Sharp just wasn't letting this go.

"We share a true and valued relationship with the American people..."

My head kept telling me the threat was over. Abe Peterson must have felt the same way, or he would be out here with his president rather than continuing to interrogate the Sudanese imposter. Clearly, he trusted his team to protect Blake while he gleaned more information from Bahri. It was a matter of prioritizing. He couldn't be in two places at once. Despite, or perhaps because of that, my own senses remained on alert.

The sniper's eye.

"So, thank you, Mr. President, for your generosity, your hospitality and your friendship. I would now like to present you with a small gift."

Again, applause filled the garden. The two presidents made their way over to the front of our stage. As prearranged, the Marine Band played a majestic fanfare as the presidents strode forward. For a last time, I scanned every face. There was no one who I could positively or even possibly say looked like Atha Riek's brother. At least not by appearance. Jefferson Blake's risky plan to call the terrorist out in person was a washout.

On cue from the MC, three members of the Sudanese party stood and headed toward the stage. The two men walked either side of a tall woman in a flowing, gold formal gown. I hadn't noticed her earlier, if I had I would have remembered, she was stunning. Head held high, black folds of hair cascading over her shoulders, her beauty was captivating as she strolled forward. An agile cat, gracefully prowling high on a rooftop. The presidents advanced toward us, Secret Service agents flanking them. The four agents focused their attentions away from their subjects, casting their eyes in a continual sweep across the crowd.

As the three Sudanese moved closer to the presentation area, and the lyre, I studied the two men. They walked with a regimented gate, like soldiers. I figured them to be bodyguards. That meant they may be a threat... or maybe just bodyguards.

The two presidents arrived in front of us, waiting for one of the Sudanese to pass the gift. The woman in gold reached the stage. As she leaned forward to take the instrument, she peeked across the platform toward the Sudanese president. He offered her a warm smile. For an instant, the women in gold hesitated, but then it was gone. She turned back and picked up the lyre, glancing up at me just as the stage lights lit her face.

That was the moment I knew we were in trouble.

Chapter 40

The grace of a cat; Al Fahad, the Leopard.

We'd got it wrong. So very wrong.

I raised my arm to yell into my sleeve mic. It was a wasted gesture. The Secret Service had turned it off, its proximity to the sound equipment interfering with their frequency.

The woman in gold must have noticed my reaction. She sped up her pace. A frantic look across the front of the stage confirmed there was no weapon in sight. Just music gear. Then I saw it. Sua'd Bahri's violin bow lay half-hidden at the foot of her chair. It was one of the newer models, made from carbon fiber.

In the same moment I laid eyes on the bow, the woman dropped the lyre and lunged forward.

"Blake, down!"

Jefferson Blake must have heard me over the band, but the Secret Service men didn't. They remained focused on threats coming from the audience.

A look of confusion crossed the president's face, his eyes searching for understanding.

My Hammond organ stood between the woman and me. I wasn't sure exactly what she was intending, but I didn't plan on waiting to find out. Leaping onto the organ, I used it as a springboard to vault the ten feet toward her.

I didn't make it.

The woman tugged on the end of the bow. Out of nowhere, a long carbon-fiber blade appeared in her hand, its smooth surface glistening under the lights. She swung the knife high, slashing through the air toward me. Its sharp edge cut like a surgeon's scalpel through the skin on my right shoulder as she drove it upward.

"You are too late," she spat.

She withdrew the blade and whirled back toward the two presidents. Blake, realizing the urgency of the situation, moved to put himself between the assassin and the Sudanese leader. Damn presidential hero.

As I lay bleeding on the edge of the stage, my muscles swimming in pain, I saw the Secret Service agents turn. They drew their SIG Sauer pistols from their holsters as they pivoted, but it was too late. They wouldn't get a shot. When Blake ran to protect the Sudanese president, he'd put himself between the agents and the woman.

I'd almost made it to my feet when a freight train collided with the side of my face. The power of the Shararaa bodyguard's blow sent me plummeting back to the floor of the stage. Suddenly, I was seeing two US presidents and two women with freakin' long knives. A dazed second later, one of the woman's bodyguards collapsed next to me as he took a round to the rear of his head. One down, but not enough.

The distraction had given the woman all the time she needed. As she raised the blade in her right hand, she stepped forward and plunged it down toward the US president's face. He saw it coming and feinted to the right. Another wasted gesture. This woman was a professional; she'd never intended to hit Blake's face. In a powerful sweep, she followed the feint, aiming the blade lower, toward the president's chest.

I was too slow to stop her, but I sure as hell wasn't giving up that easily. Using my one working arm, I pushed forward, throwing all my bodyweight in the assassin's direction. I connected with her shoulder just as the blade tore into Blake's shirt. She toppled to the left, her knife arm falling with her, but it wasn't enough. The stiletto sliced through the silk and plunged deep into the president's torso. He grunted in agony.

As the woman and I hit the ground together. She yanked the knife from the president's flailing body, and faster than I thought possible, had it at my throat. I felt the blade pierce my skin as I attempted to roll underneath her. Trapped under her weight, I struggled to release my uninjured arm. Then, reaching frantically, grabbing at anything I could find, my fingers touched the base of a microphone stand that had fallen from the stage. I snatched it up and pounded her hard on the side of her head. As she slid off me, the knife skimmed across the skin on my neck.

Another gunshot snapped through the air. At first, I thought an agent had shot the woman, but no. The second Shararaa bodyguard went down. Why in God's name hadn't they targeted the damn woman?

Then I had the answer I didn't want.

The woman in gold had rolled with the blow. Now, perched on a single knee, blood streaming from her head, she held a strangle grip on the US president's neck. He wheezed noisily as he gasped for air. The woman's other hand gripped the stiletto, poised an inch above Blake's heart. There was no clean shot that would take out the assassin without risking the president.

"No one move, don't even breathe," instructed the woman.

We all stopped. With half the Secret Service aiming their weapons at her, the gold dress turning crimson red, she didn't recoil at all. A cold killing machine.

For a split second, I thought that surely she must realize it's over.

"Bear witness to your president's harrowing death—a fitting end for my brother's murderer. Where are your apostles of freedom now?"

Her fingers tightened around her weapon, her shoulders hunched forward as she drew back the blade an inch.

"Die, damn you," she hissed, plunging the blade downward. It was over.

Kaitlin Reed's blond hair flooded my vision as she hurled herself from the back of the stage onto the woman. I didn't even know she was there. The two bodies rolled off the president, entwined in a struggling, violent mess.

The assassin broke free first, shoving Kaitlin away, causing her to fall backward onto the stage, knocking her head hard against a speaker.

The woman whirled, diving behind Blake's prone body just as several rounds of gunfire shattered the stage behind her, missing Kaitlin's motionless form by inches.

Once again, I lunged forward, attempting to separate the woman from the president. As she raised her blade for a second attempt at the kill shot, I was only inches away. Unexpectedly, the woman changed tactic. Flipping up to a half-crouch, she bore down on me. She was good, and fast... too damn fast. In my bid to help Blake, I'd now put myself between the woman and the Secret Service agents, although I was certain they'd be swarming around to find the clear shot.

The stiletto was heading my way again, and I was running out of strength. As the assassin's arm came down toward my chest, I made a last effort. Grabbing her wrist, I twisted hard with every bit of force I could summon. I felt the bone snap as I turned her knife wrist backward on a one-eighty-degree angle. The weight of the woman's torso followed through on her attack, committed. Without me shifting the weapon any further, the razor-sharp stiletto plunged straight through her heart. She collapsed onto me, her yellow eyes frozen in lifeless surprise.

Atha Riek's twin sister was dead.

Chapter 41

"I told you from the start it was a terrible idea," said Abe Peterson.

"Now just calm down, my friend. It all worked out, didn't it?" Always the voice of reason, President Jefferson Blake sat up in his hospital bed, a reassuring grin on his face.

"With all due respect, sir, you're not the one who had to do the worrying."

"Abe, you and I have known each other for a long time," said the president. "Would you expect me to act any differently?"

"No, sir, I wouldn't," replied a chastened Peterson. "I just wish this conversation wasn't taking place in a hospital room at Walter Reed Medical Center. I would have preferred a fireside chat at the White House."

"They've patched me up pretty well," said Blake. "Thanks to Nicholas, Atha Riek's sister missed all the essential organs, and thanks to Kaitlin, she didn't get another shot. They tell me I'll be back at work within three weeks."

Blake paused, his mouth widening to a fully-fledged smile as he gazed at his old friend. "And if your men hadn't taken out the Shararaa bodyguards... Nicholas and I would have been in a lot of trouble."

"Well, sir, we weren't about to lose our second president to the same terrorists in as many months."

They'd lost me.

"Tell them, Abe—they deserve to know," commanded Blake.

"The final analysis of the toxicology screens from President Carlton's autopsy showed very faint traces of ouabain. It's a cardiac glycoside that induces the symptoms of cardiac arrest."

"He was poisoned?" asked Greatrex.

"Nothing that we can prove," replied Peterson.

"The thing is," began the president, "this ouabain is commonly found in eastern Africa. Traditionally, it's used as an arrow poison."

"Are you saying the Shararaa had already taken out one president before the attack on you at the White House?" I inquired. "I'm afraid it is so," responded Jumaa, as he stared vacantly out the window. "I have never been more ashamed of my heritage. The fact that our previous government allowed the Shararaa to survive, even flourish, is beyond me."

"As the president says, we've got no proof and probably never will. However, our analysts believe it to be the case," Abe Peterson responded.

"And without proof, the public will never be told," said the president. His eyes scrutinized every individual in the room. "Is that perfectly clear?"

Nobody argued.

The president continued to speak. "Nicholas, you and Jack have risked your lives throughout this entire affair. Abe tells me that if you hadn't reacted as you did, both in recognizing Atha Riek's sister and taking her on, chances are I would have been the shortest serving president since William Henry Harrison."

"The moment I saw her eyes, it was like staring into Al

Fahad's cold soul all over again. But really, sir, I did very little."

Jefferson Blake looked straight through me.

"Bullshit," he interjected. "I thank you, my friend… for my life. Your father would be proud."

Standing by the door, Kaitlin Reed chuckled.

Greatrex changed the subject. "Abe, have you found out any more about Atha Riek's sister? Her name? How she stayed so well hidden? How she rose undetected through the government's ranks?"

Peterson responded. "Her name was Akifa Deng. We completely missed that Atha Riek sibling could be a sister—wasn't even on our radar."

"Regarding how she remained so well hidden and became so powerful, perhaps I can answer that," interrupted Jumaa.

"Go on," said Peterson.

"I have had my people in Sudan working on this. President Sabbir has been most supportive and offered every resource. He feels terrible that President Blake nearly lost his life at the hands of a Sudanese national… again.

"It appears the father was, as we expected, the motivating force behind Riek and Deng's despicable careers. The thing that baffled us was that the father lacked any real political clout. He was a heavy-handed and violent man, sending in his daughter to infiltrate the government just wasn't his style."

"So how did she find her way?" I asked.

"Apparently she had a mentor," continued Jumaa. "Someone high up enough in the government ranks to create a pathway for her. Someone who shared enough of the Shararaa's beliefs to risk everything."

"You mean some sort of sociopathic sponsor?" added

Greatrex.

"Precisely, Jack. Shall I go on, sir?" Jumaa looked directly at the president.

Blake just nodded.

"The story goes that once Akifa Deng showed an incredible talent for manipulation, her mentor realized she was bound for far greater career heights than his own."

"So?" I asked.

"So, once she reached an elevated position, and he could do no more for her, he simply disappeared. Officials can find no trace of the man. They don't know what name he goes by now or where he is. To be honest, even if they knew his identity, they have no proof of his crimes. Our new president demands transparency. He refuses to oversee a police state where individuals just disappear. He believes his country should now be free of that style of government."

"They are admirable aspirations in a leader," said Jefferson Blake. "The trouble is that this man has caused immeasurable pain to so many innocent people, yet no one can do a thing about it."

"It's almost like being back to square one," added Greatrex. There was an edge in his voice.

"Almost," said Jumaa. "As the Secret Service investigators went through Deng's belongings, they found a photo. Perhaps it remained her single weakness—an attachment she couldn't give up. Maybe this man had even been the covert conduit to her brother."

"Do you have a copy?" I asked.

"I do—Agent Peterson provided me with it," replied our Sudanese friend. He reached into his pocket and produced a picture. Greatrex took it first, scanned it and without saying

a word passed it to me.
  I was surprised.

Epilogue

The wind had grown colder since we'd last been here. The rolling spaces between the foothills of the Batn-El-Hajar Mountains allowed the chilly air to move unimpeded across the plains.

"Are you sure about this?" I asked.

"Yes, my friend. Bloodlines in Sudan can be complicated and convoluted, but shared blood does not forgive evil." Jumaa gazed down to the landscape below, his head tilted to one side. He continued, speaking in a slow, measured tone. "I love my sister and I loved her husband, Aathif, as though he was my own brother. He *was* my brother. We dreamed together, and then suddenly, thanks to these bastards, I witnessed the life drain from his soul before my eyes. I felt the anguish in my sister's heart when I told her that her son has no father. We must stop these Shararaa assassins. Sadly, I disagree with my president on how that is done... in this instance."

"This won't bring anyone back," said Greatrex, lying on the sand behind the same rocky outcrop as Jumaa and I.

"I know, but no one else will die by his hand."

We stared down into the valley and waited.

If there were demons to deal with, I would deal with them later.

Eventually, an aging white pick-up pulled up in front of the low set clay-and-stone building. It parked in the same spot where Greatrex and I had waited impatiently for Jumaa several months before, as we searched for the Shararaa camp.

The old man got out. He drew his robes tighter to protect himself from the wind. He had nothing to fear out here. This was his county, his people. His nephew never understood that. He was getting cold now and knew he should go inside. There were fresh plans to rebuild the brotherhood. He would be part of them. Despite the service he'd already given to the cause, the old man still possessed the energy... and the faith, whatever that meant.

He had time for one more look around. For a split second, in the distance, a thousand yards away, he noticed a glint of metal in the fading sun.

It was the last thing he ever saw.

Afterword

Get your FREE electronic copy of the NICHOLAS SHARP origins Novella PLAY OUT, the latest news about new releases and some other exciting freebies along the way by joining my mailing list at my website: https://markm annock.com

Although you can begin reading the NICHOLAS SHARP THRILLER series at any point here is my suggested order of reading:

PLAY OUT-an origins novella (*available exclusively to my mailing list members on sign-up*) can be read at any point. The story takes you back to when Nicholas Sharp left the U.S. Marines.

What readers are saying about the Nicholas Sharp Series:

"I had to keep reading to the end, could not put it away until I had finished."

"I love Lee Child and now have another author who is just as good."

"Jack Reacher's attitude... John Lennon's sensibilities."

"I really enjoyed the sniper-musician-reluctant warrior character..."

"I've read hundreds of books throughout the years and the pandemic has provided me with extra time to discover more reading treasures. Play Out (Nicholas Sharp Origins novella) is one of the best."

"Without a doubt this is a cracking novel... the story then keeps at you in leaps and bounds! Full of action all the way. Just brilliant!"

Reviews are life's blood to an author. If you've enjoyed KILLSONG please consider leaving a review on the book's Amazon page.

Acknowledgements

My heartfelt thanks and love to Sarah, Anisha and Jack for your love, tolerance and support. Lachlan, your counsel and wisdom is eternally appreciated. Thank you also to Rebecca Millar, my wonderful and patient editor.

To my good friend Simon Landid. Thank you for living such an inspiring life and sharing your adventures with me.

Cover by Anisha Mannock

About the Author

Mark Mannock was born in Melbourne, Australia. He has had an extensive career in the music industry including supporting, recording with or writing for Tina Turner, Joni Mitchell, The Eurythmics, Irene Cara and David Hudson. His recorded work with Lia Scallon has twice been long-listed for Grammy Awards.

As a composer/songwriter Mark's music has been used across the world in countless television and theatre contexts, including the 'American Survivor' TV series and 'Sleuth' playwright Anthony Shaffer's later productions.

Mark has also been active in music education across Australia promoting student's ownership and voice in their own educational music journeys. He has won several awards for his endeavours in this area.

Mark is presently writing the successful 'Nicholas Sharp' thriller series about a disillusioned former US sniper whose past plagues him as he makes his way in the contemporary music industry. Sharp is a man whose insatiable curiosity and embedded moral compass lead him to places he ought not go. The series is currently read in over 50 countries.

Mark lives in Kettering, Tasmania with his family. His travels around the globe act as inspirations for his writing.

Mark enjoys hearing from his readers, so please feel free to contact him.

You can connect with me on:
🌐 https://markmannock.com
f https://www.facebook.com/markmannockbooks

Subscribe to my newsletter:
✉ https://markmannock.com

Also by Mark Mannock

PLAY OUT
https://markmannock.com
A Nicholas Sharp Origin Novella

Sign up to my mailing list and receive this book for free!

Set five years before **KILLSONG**
   A Terrorist attack on the London Underground. Nicholas Sharp doesn't think so.

While on leave from Iraq, the U.S. Marine Sniper finds himself intervening when innocent lives are threatened. He walks away, but for Sharp it's never that easy. Something doesn't feel right. Twenty-four hours later everything is wrong.

The brief solace he finds in his beloved piano is shattered when Sharp becomes the attacker's next target. Step up or step away. Nicholas Sharp doesn't like to kill, but he sure as hell knows how to.

Somewhere between Tom Clancy's *Jack Ryan* and Robert Crais' *Elvis Cole*, Nicholas Sharp may be a flawed hero, but you certainly want him on your side.

"I've read hundreds of books throughout the years and the pandemic has provided me with extra time to discover more reading treasures. Play Out is one of the best." **Goodreads Reviewer-5 STARS**

The Nicholas Sharp origins novella PLAY OUT is sent to you FREE when you join my mailing list at
   https://markmannock.com

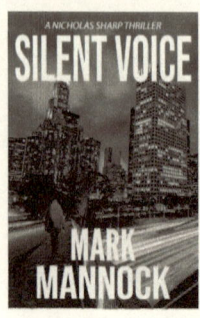

SILENT VOICE
Nicholas Sharp Thriller #4

Hunted down by their government's secret service, the members of protest band Kha Cring flee to Los Angeles to begin a new life. After an unexpected attack, the musicians' safe exile in LA is jeopardized. The desire to fight for their country's freedom undiminished, the band find their soaring popularity and politically messaged music no longer enough to protect them from the evil they escaped.

A deadlier weapon is needed. Nicholas Sharp.

In an instant things go terribly wrong as Sharp finds himself the focus of a network of international conspirators intent on wiping both he and the members of Kha Cring from the face of the planet.

Available on Amazon:
  http://www.amazon.com/dp/B08W1V9FWS
  http://www.amazon.co.uk/dp/B08W1V9FWS
  http://www.amazon.com.au/dp/B08W1V9FWS
  https://www.amazon.ca/dp/B08W1V9FWS .

COUNTERPOINT
Nicholas Sharp Thriller #5

Looking in the mirror, he saw only death...

Pursued by one of the world's most efficient and ruthless assassins, Nicholas Sharp almost admires the deadly operator's meticulous talents, until the assassin starts coming after Sharp through his friends. Sharp's investigations reveal that the killer also has another target in sight: the US Secretary of Defense. Is there a dark connection?

Face to face with a past he'd considered banished from his memory, Nicholas Sharp questions not only his own moral compass but also his slim chance of survival.

Available on Amazon:

http://www.amazon.com/dp/B0BVTVWZ6N
http://www.amazon.co.uk/dp/B0BVTVWZ6N
http://www.amazon.com.au/dp/B0BVTVWZ6N
https://www.amazon.ca/dp/B0BVTVWZ6N

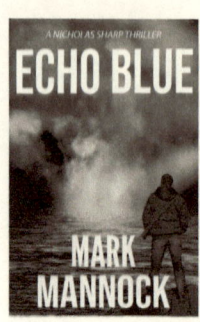

ECHO BLUE
Nicholas Sharp Thriller #6

Are you safe?...

Nicholas Sharp receives a mysterious phone call from Jack Greatrex... then Greatrex disappears.

In a hunt that takes him through South America, Texas, the mountains of Northern Spain and eventually the Middle East, Sharp encounters world renowned environmental activist Dr Deagan Jones from the notorious Crimson Wave. As Sharp uncovers a chain of complex deceptions, Jones' teenage son is kidnapped. The stakes never higher, the ex-Marine sniper turned musician fights to prevent an environmental and humanitarian catastrophe with unimaginable consequences.

Available on Amazon: (August 2023, pre-order now)
http://www.amazon.com/dp/B0BVV25R2F
http://www.amazon.co.uk/dp/B0BVV25R2F
http://www.amazon.com.au/dp/B0BVV25R2F
https://www.amazon.ca/dp/B0BVV25R2F

KILLSONG
Nicholas Sharp Thriller #1

Nicholas Sharp is a killer musician... literally!

Turning his back on the military system that turned him into a murderer when he shot an innocent man, Sharp is grateful to have found refuge in a career as a successful musician. But while he is preparing to back well-known former rock star Robbie West on a USO tour of Iraq, a close friend and her daughter disappear.

In a deadly game of cat and mouse across three continents, Sharp discovers there's more at stake than his own life and those close to him. As relentless shadows from his past chase him down, he faces a brutal choice. Kill or be killed.

"I had to keep reading to the end, could not put it away until I had finished." **Amazon Reader- 5 STARS**

"Jack Reachers attitude... John Lennon's sensibilities." **Goodreads Reviewer- 5 STARS**

Available on Amazon:
http://www.amazon.com/dp/B08CT1FHF5
http://www.amazon.co.uk/dp/B08CT1FHF5
http://www.amazon.com.au/dp/B08CT1FHF5
https://www.amazon.ca/dp/B08CT1FHF5

LETHAL SCORE
Nicholas Sharp Thriller #2

"A great book that has more twists and turns than you can imagine. Pick up and read at all costs." **Goodreads Reviewer 5 STARS**

Nicholas Sharp is on a tour through Europe, the concerts are sold out and the former Marine sniper turned musician is living in luxury thanks to promoter Antonio Ascardi.

Suddenly it all goes wrong. People are dying along the way and Sharp is blamed. Now a hunted man, accused of terrorist crimes across the continent, Nicholas Sharp must fight for his life and freedom.

Available on Amazon:
  http://www.amazon.com/dp/B08CSYKG18
  http://www.amazon.co.uk/dp/B08CSYKG18
  http://www.amazon.com.au/dp/B08CSYKG18
  https://www.amazon.ca/dp/B08CSYKG18

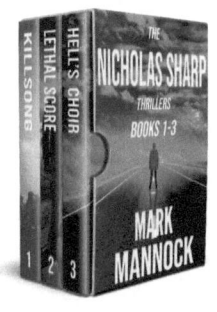

The NICHOLAS SHARP THRILLER BOOKS 1-3 BOXSET

KILLSONG

   LETHAL SCORE

   HELL'S CHOIR

   Three great Nicholas Sharp Novels in one Box Set

http://www.amazon.com/dp/B08 NYLGW1G http://www.amazon.co.uk/dp/B08NYLGW1G http://www.amazon.com.au/dp/B08NYLGW1G https://www.amazon.ca/dp/B08NYLGW1G

BLOOD NOTE

https://markmannock.com

A Short Story Prequel to the Thriller KILLSONG *(should be read after KILLSONG-available FREE to mailing list subscribers 7 days after sign-up)*

Just turn around and walk away. That was all Nicholas Sharp had to do when the mysterious and intoxicating Elena approached him for help.

She knew far too much about him. The warning signs were all there.

Sharp didn't listen to them.

What followed for the former Marine Sniper turned musician, was a harrowing night of violence, deceit and intrigue.

When the sunrise ushered in a new day, Sharp thought it was all over...but it was really just beginning.